Amethyst Chronicles

Vol 1

K.G. Stutts

Amethyst Chronicles
Volume 1
Written by KG Stutts
Cover Designed by TheWritingNetwork

MidnightRose
copyright 2015
ISBN 978-1-63310-032-9

Thank you in advance for your review.

CHAPTER ONE

Laser fire ricocheted off the steel walls the moment Ember Wilson opened a security lock. She pressed her back flat against the wall to avoid the energy blasts. The scraping of metal on metal echoed in her ears as drones approached their location.

"I thought Morris took care of the security drones?" Her second-in-command, Michael Lewis, questioned behind her.

As soon as he asked, the blaster fire from the drones stopped. A droid stood in the doorway motionless for a moment before falling over. A crackle came over their ear piece before the voice of the team's tech master, Bryan Morris, came through.

"Sorry about that," he said.

Ember rolled her eyes as she dropped out of her defensive stance. "We've got to move. Rudo knows we're here now."

"Nova has a distraction set up and ready to blow and I have hijacked the camera feed. Right now, Rudo's team is scrambling to find out why an old episode of Stargate SG-1 is on their monitors instead of the base," Morris informed her.

Lewis grinned as he moved toward the door. Morris loved the old entertainment programs from their ancestors more than anything currently available on the hologram recreational programing.

Ember brushed back a loose strain of her coal black hair as she readied for the next task. "Morris, make sure Rudo can't fix the camera feed. Nova, light it up then head back to the hangar bay. We need to be able to take off in five."

"Aye," Nova's voice acknowledged over her ear piece.

The building rumbled and shook as Nova executed his task. Rudo knew the special ops team known as Amethyst was there, but as long as her tech guru had his lock on the security, no one knew where they were.

"At least we still have the element of surprise," Lewis said.

She nodded and opened the second door on the engineering level of Clayton Rudo's impregnable fortress in Texas. Nothing was going to deter her from the mission. Knowing what she was about to do would brand her a traitor, she still pressed forward. Perhaps one day, the people would thank her.

For centuries, Earth had been ravaged by harsh winters, hurricanes, droughts, and blistering summers. For the last ten years, the bulk of Earth's food was grown on other worlds. Then Clayton Rudo, a scientist working with the Intergalactic Security Commission's home base in West Virginia, announced he had a plan. He had created a machine which would regulate the weather systems. He promised Earth would return to the lush land it was in the history archives.

But Ember had discovered the truth. Recently Morris had decrypted the real plan. Rudo planned to take over and rule, not cure the soil. No, Clayton Rudo was not the humanitarian everyone believed him to be.

She went to General Tom Blanchard with the news. And he dismissed her.

The area was clear as they raced through a long walkway. The sound of heavy boots alerted them to the fact they were no longer alone as they rounded a corner.

"Get them!" Rudo's men yelled as a group of four henchmen spotted Ember and Lewis.

"Sorry, don't have time for this," Ember said.

Lewis dodged blaster fire as Ember launched herself into the air. The foot soldiers stared agape as she soared over them, landing gracefully behind them. Lewis threw a flash grenade, blinding the enemies. The group yelled and fell to their knees, covering their eyes. By the time their vision returned, Ember and Lewis were long gone.

"Wilson, what's your status?" Morris asked.

"Headed into the weather system room."

"I picked up a comm moments ago. General Blanchard is here."

She swore under her breath before acknowledging. Of course, the presence of the only active five star general in the Air Force would complicate matters.

"We're out of time," Ember stated, grabbing Lewis by the arm.

An alarm started blaring, painting the area in a red light. Ember and Lewis sprinted down the hall, fighting their way to their targeted destination. Laser fire filled the air as the two kept at their relentless pace.

They took down several men before Lewis threw a frag grenade as he ducked around a corner. Screams and debris filled the air. The smell of blood and burnt flesh mingled as the ventilation system activated as they continued on their quest.

"No time to wait on Morris," Ember said before blasting the security console to the weather computer room.

Lewis pulled back the heavy door and the duo was immediately under fire.

"Go!" he yelled, covering for her.

She knew General Blanchard would order for her team to be taken alive. She was counting on his sympathies. A small grin tugged on the corner of her mouth when she got her confirmation. The blasters were emitting a green light, signaling the setting was on stun, not kill. It would take a ton of power to render them unconscious, buying her just enough time for her to accomplish her goal. Lewis drew fire away from Ember as she set C4 charges on the computer console. She readied the detonator in her hand.

"Morris, do you read?" she asked.

"I hear you. What's going on?"

"Are you sure you have the research files?"

"Positive."

"Wilson, what the hell are you waiting for?" Lewis hollered.

She pressed her lips into a thin line as the last of her explosives was placed. Her brow crinkled when she heard a loud groan. Looking slightly over her shoulder, she saw Lewis had finally been subdued by Rudo's operatives. Several of them fired a stun blast at her. The first few shots she was able to shake off.

"Ember," a stern voice said from behind.

Her entire body froze when she recognized the voice of General Blanchard. The moment she turned around, he fired twice directly into her chest. Her body began to tingle, but she didn't go down. However, another shot would render her unconscious. There was a limit to what her body could absorb. It didn't matter what happened to her, though. Her mission was complete. She gave him a slight smile and pressed the red trigger button, causing the weather system computer to explode. Computer parts and glass flew across the room as everyone ducked for cover.

"What have you done?" General Blanchard bellowed when the building shook again.

"What you weren't man enough to do yourself." Her voice was void of emotion.

His brow furrowed as he raised his weapon again. He fired another shot into her chest. This time, she dropped down to her knees as her strength began to leave her body and she convulsed. The room spun as she collapsed, falling unconscious.

***

Major Liam Ross wasn't sure what to think when he received orders to meet with General Tom Blanchard. Not a lot of information was given. Still, if it was important enough to be invited to Blanchard's space station, Lunis Two, he didn't question it. As soon as he landed in the docking bay, he was greeted by a pretty redheaded woman. Her eyes raked over him appreciatively as he removed his hat and ran a hand through his short brown hair. He squared his broad shoulders back, the fabric of his dress military uniform straining against his muscles.

He stood at attention. "Major Liam Ross reporting to General Tom Blanchard."

"Major Ross, I am General Blanchard's personal secretary, Ashlee Figiel," she greeted, licking her lips. "Right this way."

He followed her through the corridors of the space station. Lunis Two was designed to be the cornerstone in the latest military operations. The newest technology was housed here. Ashlee pulled him along, not letting him linger for any length of time. She came to a stop outside a pair of double doors and entered in a code to unlock it. He raised an eyebrow, but quickly dismissed it. Everyone was under a heightened state of awareness lately. Of course security protocol would limit access to the General. Ashlee smiled sweetly as she ushered him in to meet with the general who was sitting at an office desk.

General Blanchard was a man in his late fifties with graying black hair of military length and wrinkles underneath his serious brown eyes. He looked slightly disheveled even in his clean uniform. Liam stood at attention and cleared his voice when the General failed to address him. Blanchard looked up, taking a sip from his coffee cup before getting to his feet.

"General Blanchard, sir." Major Ross saluted.

"At ease, Major." The General offered his hand.

"Thank you, sir." Ross shook it.

"You're probably wondering why you're here," Blanchard said.

"Yes, sir."

"Walk with me."

General Blanchard pulled a large painting of him and his daughter, Laura, from a wall and revealed a security key pad. He punched in a security code and motioned Ross over. A portion of the wall gave way to reveal a secret room. The room looked like a lab with white walls, a gray marble floor, and various computers and equipment he didn't recognize. Against the back wall were four pods with people asleep in stasis.

The General stood in front of the first pod, stroking his unkempt bearded chin. The sleeping man had extremely short black hair and was the shortest and skinniest of the four in the tubes. As they approached, a holographic image appeared on the glass next to the man's face. The picture was of a smiling man with wire-rimmed glasses on his thin nose, brown eyes, and longer hair.

"This is Bryan Morris," the General introduced. "Best tech man I've ever seen. Smart, quick on his feet, and crafty."

Liam looked at the General curiously, but he didn't elaborate further. Blanchard moved down to the next pod. The man inside was slightly taller than Morris and had curly red hair. The holographic picture displayed another smiling man with light blue eyes and hair sticking out everywhere.

"Alexander Nova. He was the best pilot Earth had to offer. And this," the General pointed to the third tube, "is Michael Lewis. Brilliant military mind. He was second-in-command."

Ross wrinkled up his nose as he gazed upon the strong specimen of a man. Lewis was tall and clearly well-built with brown hair that stopped just above his eyebrows. The image displayed was of a serious man with brown eyes.

"Command?" Ross questioned, but the General didn't address it.

He moved down to the last pod which had a woman in it. Ross looked at the tall woman with jet black hair who was somehow scowling even though she was asleep. The picture showed a strikingly beautiful blonde woman with blue eyes.

"Ember Wilson," General Blanchard softly said. "She's the leader of this team known as Amethyst."

His voice pulled Liam's attention away from her. "Amethyst, sir?"

"A group of genetically enhanced super soldiers. They were Earth's greatest defense."

"I've never heard of Amethyst."

"Nor would you. The gene program was top secret. They were named after a side effect of the genetic manipulation causing the quartet's eye color to change to a brilliant shade of dark purple."

"Gene program? Purple eyes? Sir, this is a little unbelievable."

"They had it all," General Blanchard continued, still not answering the Major's questions. "Super strength, speed, endurance, skill, stamina, healing, and intelligence. They could withstand several kill blaster shots before they even felt a twinge to their central nervous system. Their natural talents increased tenfold."

Liam let out a low whistle. "What happened? What led them here?"

"You remember two years ago when the weather computer designed by Clayton Rudo was destroyed?"

Liam nodded. Of course he remembered. Rudo was proclaimed a hero when he introduced a super computer that could control Earth's climate.

"Ember came to me and said Rudo had plans to control Earth, but I didn't believe her. As a result, Amethyst attacked Rudo's lab in Abilene and destroyed the system."

"They were the ones behind the assault? Sir, I helped designed the security protocol for Dr. Rudo's base myself."

"I'm aware, Major. I haven't met a security platform which Amethyst couldn't disable. Because of their actions, they were on trial for treason and convicted. Due to the team's enhanced abilities, it was decreed they would remain in stasis until they could be rehabilitated."

"But we later found out she was right."

"Yes. Of course it would take us two years to realize. It took, but Rudo rebuilt his machine. I even assigned several top scientists to help speed the process along after Amethyst thoroughly destroyed all of his work. And now ..."

And now Rudo used his weather system to bring the world to its knees. Washington, D.C., New Mexico, and Texas were now completely under ice. Everything was frozen solid.

General Blanchard turned away from the sleeping woman. For a split second, the Major thought he saw a mixture of sadness and sorrow in the other man's eyes before going back to normal.

"They are Earth's only hope to stop Rudo once and for all."

"If that's true, then why am I here?" Liam asked.

"Before the President went into his underground bunker, he ordered me to assemble the best military team to work alongside of Amethyst. You are the leader of my team, Major."

"If Amethyst is so great, then why do you need me?"

"President Packer believes the team is too unpredictable now. We can't guarantee they will help us after everything that's happened."

"You mean, after you ignored the warning then placed them in stasis tubes?"

The General raised an eyebrow. "Yes, that's what I mean. They defied direct orders."

"Sir, I'm not going to babysit a bunch of medically altered--"

"Major Ross, these are your orders," General Blanchard sternly said. "Your squad is to work with Amethyst to eradicate the threat to save our planet and billions of lives."

"Yes, sir."

***

He wasn't happy about it, but orders were orders. Liam watched as one by one members of Amethyst were taken out of stasis except for Ember Wilson.

Michael Lewis staggered out of the stasis chamber. He rubbed his eyes as he quickly recovered from the sleep effects. Ross' eyes widened in surprise at the unnatural shade of purple they were. Blanchard wasn't kidding about the violet eyes.

Lewis glared and balled his hands into fists as he locked eyes on General Blanchard.

"You have some nerve -"

"I'm aware," the General cut him off. "But you are needed."

"What makes you think Wilson or any of us will help you after you dumped us in here?" Lewis demanded.

"Because she was right," Blanchard stated.

"Ah." Lewis looked amused. "So Rudo activated the weather system after all. I shouldn't gloat about the fact Rudo did what Wilson told you he would, but I just can't help myself."

"Gloating isn't going to help matters."

"Yeah, that may be true, but it sure is fun."

The General's eyes narrowed but he didn't lose his composure. Nova and Morris were recovering from their stasis sleep and the trio was brought up to speed on Rudo.

"You silly, stupid old man," Morris seethed, bitterness resonating in his voice. "If you had listened to Wilson when she told you-"

"I'm well aware, Mr. Morris," the General said, his irritation beginning to show. "But what's done is done. Now I need your help to make it right."

"How long?" Morris inquired.

"Two years."

Nova chuckled. "We really did a number on his base."

"Apparently not good enough," Morris grumbled.

"You know she's going to be livid when she wakes," Nova said.

"Of course he does." Lewis snorted. "Why else do you think he reanimated us first? He knows she would put a hole in his head the first chance she got."

Nova laughed. "You think we're going to help keep Wilson subdued?"

"I'm hoping to reason with her," Blanchard replied.

"Reason?" Morris questioned. "You mean like when she told you what Rudo was planning to do and you dismissed her? Then you tried and convicted her of criminal charges?"

"Yeah, and now when she's proven right, he thinks we're just going to fall in line." Nova rolled his eyes as he leaned against a stasis chamber.

"Clayton Rudo was a benevolent scientist who claimed to have the means to save our planet." Blanchard defended.

"You were desperate and acted accordingly." Lewis countered.

"We all were! Is it so wrong to want something to believe in?"

"You mean, like a father believing in his daughter?" Nova asked.

The other two men whistled low at the dig. General Blanchard's brown eyes flashed as he balled up his fists.

Nova chuckled. "Temper, temper, General."

"Leave my personal life out of it."

"What personal life? The blonde princess you parade around as your only daughter and pretend your first born doesn't exist?" Lewis inquired.

"Wait, this woman is your daughter?" Liam pointed to the fourth pod.

Lewis looked him up and down before rolling his eyes. "I'm not surprised you left that key part out, General. You must be ashamed. Question is, do you regret having a daughter who stands up for what's right, even if it means challenging you, or does it eat you up inside knowing she was right and you ruined her life?"

"That's enough," Blanchard snapped.

"The truth hurts, General." Nova shrugged. Suddenly he stood up straight and began checking his pockets. "Ah, man. I'm out of gum."

"Forget your gum," Lewis grumbled. "Focus."

"It'd be easier to focus if I had gum."

"All right." Morris clapped his hands together. "As much as it pains me to say anything in support of General Windbag, Earth is in trouble if Rudo has activated his machine."

The trio looked at each other and nodded in agreement.

"Wake Ember," Lewis ordered. "We'll do it."

It was the first time Liam had heard anyone refer to the woman by her first name. The dynamic of the group intrigued him. Admiration and an edge of danger mixed in their voices when they spoke of their leader. A part of him wondered just what he was getting into with this group. Thankfully the trio seemed to disregard the Major completely, probably thinking he was there to act as muscle in case Wilson got out of control. If that was the case, they were only partially right.

A lab technician carefully brought Ember Wilson out of stasis. Liam stood back as her team surrounded the final pod. Her violet eyes fluttered open and Liam's hands began to shake. He couldn't believe how stunning she was.

"What the hell?" she groaned.

"You'll feel sick to your stomach for a moment, but it will pass," Lewis informed her.

"My head," she muttered, rubbing her temple. "What did that empty-headed, bureaucrat ass kisser Blanchard to do to me? How long have we been out?"

"Two years," he replied.

"Wilson, take a second to get your bearings," Morris said.

"You'll feel back to normal in a moment," Nova added.

She scanned the lab, coming to a stop the moment her eyes locked on the General. Her foot pressed against the back of the pod, her eyes wild with anger.

"You son of a bitch!" she yelled as she used her foot to launch herself in the air.

Nova and Morris caught her before she could reach Blanchard. She kicked and screamed for freedom but the duo wouldn't budge. She jerked against the hold they had on her arms, spitting and cursing.

"I know," Lewis calmly said as he stood in front of her. Her foot was inches from his chin when she kicked. "Hey, it's okay. I know. But there are more pressing matters at hand than him."

"Rudo?" she asked through gritted teeth.

"You got it."

"You moron!" she shouted, looking over Lewis' shoulder to Blanchard. "You had the chance to stop it before he could act but you were too much of a coward!"

"I'm sorry--"

"Sorry? Sorry?" Her voice was nearly shrieking. "Not yet, but you will be."

"Wilson, Rudo used the weather machine," Nova stated, his face contorted as he strained to keep his hold on her.

"Of course he did! And now we've got to clean up the mess."

"Whatever problems you and I have aren't important right now," Blanchard said.

"You got that right," she snapped. "I'm going to finish what I started and kill Rudo and maybe you'll be lucky not to meet my blaster."

"There's no cause for that," Liam spoke up.

Her purple eyes looked upon the Major for the first time. He instantly regretted interrupting. She stopped struggling against Nova and Morris. A low growl rumbled from deep in her throat as her eyes narrowed. He shifted uncomfortably, fidgeting with the hem of his dress blues. The coldness in her eyes made him shiver.

"Who's the uniform?" She nodded in his direction.

"This is Major Liam Ross," Blanchard introduced. "His team will be working with yours on this mission."

"Absolutely not." Ember shook her head as Nova and Morris let go of her arms. "We're all you need."

"President Packer disagrees."

"I don't give a flying monkey's butt what Packer says."

"This is bigger than your raid on Rudo. You need the man power."

"No one else could've broken into the compound! We don't need or want the help."

"It doesn't matter."

"Doesn't matter." Ember fumed. "In case you've forgotten, we don't work well with others."

"I know. The leader of the Luteus team still isn't one hundred percent after the skirmish your two teams had."

"It was a training exercise. Besides, if Mark is still healing after all this time, he should spend time in a therapy tank. That's not my problem."

"Regardless of how you feel, this is the situation. Or you can be put back into the stasis chamber."

"Not on your life." Ember's lips twitched.

"Glad we've reached an accord." Blanchard nodded.

Wilson turned to Ross again, sizing him up. He was tall and, judging by the way his Air Force blues molded to him, was very muscular. His brown hair framed his handsome face but didn't touch the collar of his impeccably clean uniform. Soft brown eyes were watching her intensely.

"Can your pretty boy even hold a blaster?" She questioned Blanchard, nodding toward Liam.

"Direct your inquiries toward me." Liam stood up straighter.

Ember raised an eyebrow, looking slightly amused. "Oh, yeah?"

"I'll have you know that I'm the number one ranking sharpshooter in the world," he told her.

"It's cute you think like that. Rankings don't mean shit," she said. "Scores on a piece of paper are useless in the field."

"I assure you, Major Ross and his five squad members are more than capable of the task," the General said.

"Five?" The members of Amethyst began to laugh.

"You need a squad of five?" Ember chuckled. "Rookie."

"You only need three on your team?" Liam incredulously asked.

"I only need two, but Nova grew on me."

"Aw, thanks, Wilson." Nova grinned. "That may be the nicest thing you've ever said to me."

Ember's eyes burned into the Major's as she continued to assess him.

"All right, pretty boy. Let's see what you and your boys can do," she said. "Collect your squad and meet us in the training center."

CHAPTER TWO

Amethyst was already in the training center when Ross arrived with his squad. The quartet seemed unimpressed by the Air Force team in their fatigues. They looked thoroughly military trained which to Ember meant they didn't have a creative thought between them. All rules and regulations. The perfect soldier.

She scowled. Of course her father would assign a bunch of boy scouts for this mission.

"Kevin McKnight, Henry Lassiter, Corey Johnston, Robert Martin, and Conner Walsh," Major Liam Ross said, introducing his team and gesturing to each member in turn.

Kevin McKnight blushed as he was introduced. He was short and lean with dirty blond hair and green eyes. Henry Lassiter waved at her. He was a man of average height and build, albeit plain looking. Ember rolled her eyes as he grinned at her. Corey Johnston was incredibly tall, towering over all the other men in the room. He was bald with a full beard. Conner Walsh was a chubby man with red curly hair and blue eyes. Ember wondered if he was over the military weight limit.

"There's no way I'm going to remember your names," Ember stated.

Liam pressed his lips together in a thin line. "Are you even going to try to cooperate with the General's orders?"

"Not likely."

Liam sighed. "Come on, men. Let's show her what we're made of."

Among the science labs and military offices, the Lunis Two space station was fully equipped with a martial arts studio, a shooting range, and training simulators. The training room was Ember's favorite place to be in the station. Dozens of silver stripes, which housed thousands of microscopic holographic projectors and sensors, lined the black walls. On a separate wall hung a computer console. Next to the console was a line of various handheld weapons of different weights and lengths. The upper level of the training room housed a gallery to view the sessions so the instructors could survey the cadets as they train without distraction. The Amethyst team went into the viewing gallery and watched Ross' team activate one of the hologram simulator programs.

"Children," Lewis said as they watched the military team spread out. Ember nodded in agreement.

The chosen training program was designed to recreate a battlefield. The black walls disappeared as the computer created a realistic looking city torn apart by a war. Below them, Amethyst could hear the crumbling of buildings and painful cries as a horde of robots attacked. The goal of the exercise was to incapacitate the robot enemies and save twelve civilians.

"How much time do you think?" Nova asked.

"I'd give it fifteen minutes," Lewis said.

"Under ten minutes before Major Tight-pants is alone," Ember chimed in.

Morris chuckled. "I bet a lithium bar they are all eliminated in twelve."

"I'll take that bet," Nova said. "What are the odds someone will bleed within five?"

"Safety protocols are in place to avoid that," Morris replied.

"I know but this group looks like they would figure out a way to gush blood."

"Platinum bar says they don't save all the hologram people," Morris said.

"Look at you throwing out lithium and platinum bars," Ember mused, not taking her eyes off the field.

"I've invested wisely."

Lewis grinned. "Two pounds of chocolate says the chubby one drops his blaster."

"That's not nice." Ember clicked her tongue at him. "But a gold bar says he's the first one stunned."

"You're on."

Several of the Air Force servicemen quickly became overwhelmed. They scurried around the field, trying to formulate a plan. No one dropped their weapons, but the one Ember pegged did get knocked out first. Lewis sighed and said she would get the bar after dinner. Eight minutes into the training exercise, five of the military personnel were stunned. Major Ross was alone with only three civilians saved and a platoon of robots after him.

"He doesn't stand a chance," Morris said.

Ember leaned forward in her chair, her elbows resting on her knees. Her eyes focused on the Major, curious about his plan.

"You can learn a lot about someone by watching them fight," she said. "Pretense doesn't matter in a battle."

The Major proved to be smart, resourceful, and fast with a blaster. He managed to rescue eight of the civilians on his own.

"He's good. I mean, damn good," Nova noted.

"Probably better than Lewis." Morris teased.

Lewis elbowed Morris in the ribs. "Not a chance."

Ross was stunned to the ground as he attempted to save the last person, ending the simulation. Amethyst descended on the field as the computer quit projecting the fake city. The military squad gathered around them, looking battered from the trial.

"Not bad," Ember said.

"Not bad?" One of them with the name Lassiter on his jacket echoed. "I had never taken part of a simulation like it."

"Yeah, like you could do better," another one, McKnight, scoffed.

"We can and we have," Nova bragged.

"Prove it," Walsh said.

Ember grinned but there was no amusement behind it. "Stand back, ladies. You don't want to get hurt."

***

Once Amethyst was alone on the field, Ember gave the order to start the exercise. The computer filled in the space around them, recreating the earlier exercise.

"Lewis, you're with me," she ordered. "Nova and Morris, save the kids."

Nova and Morris sprinted off to where they could hear cries for help. Ember charged her battery pack on her blaster as Lewis pressed his back into hers. They waited until several enemies had discovered their location. Ember launched herself in the air, landing on the shoulders of an approaching robot. It tried to toss her off, but she reached under the metal collar and pulled out several wires. She rolled forward as it fell to the ground.

Lewis blasted the mechanical head off another robot as Ember blew a hole through the stomach of one that tried to grab her. The duo continued in tandem, disabling the enemies around them in less than seven minutes. Nova and

Morris converged on their location, grinning ear to ear. The simulation came to an end.

"You guys are fantastic!" the guy with the name Johnston exclaimed.

"Barely broke a sweat." Lewis shrugged.

"Come on, guys. Let's get something to eat," Morris suggested.

Lewis and Ember held back as the others went to the mess hall. A small smirk tugged at the corner of her mouth as Lewis pulled two bamboo swords from the wall of weapons next to the console. She rolled her shoulders back as she felt the weight of the shinai weapon in her hands.

"Think you can hang?" he asked.

Ember raised an eyebrow as she tapped the end of the bamboo cane on the floor. She held the stick just above her right shoulder, her left arm bent defensively at her stomach.

Lewis swung his stick at her midsection which she casually blocked. The duo circled each other a few times before he swiped at her ankles. Their weapons knocked as she parried the strike. She swung up and connected the tip of her stick against his wrist. Lewis dropped back, swearing under his breath as he cradled his wrist against his stomach. Her lips curled into a snarl as she advanced toward him.

The sound of the wood cracking echoed in the training room. Lewis pushed off against her cane and struck her wrist.

"Now we're even," he said.

"Not for long," she taunted, continuing her assault.

He raised his stick over his head and swung, connecting against her shoulder. She winced and landed a strong kick to his midsection. Lewis fell to the ground. Ember was favoring her shoulder but still managed to disarm him.

"I win." She flashed a smile.

***

Watching Amethyst destroy the training simulation made Major Liam Ross incredibly nervous. His team was completely outclassed by the quartet. Doubt filled his mind as Ember dismantled a robot in one swift motion.

Unbeknown to them, he hung back in the observation deck as Ember Wilson and Michael Lewis continued their exercise with bamboo swords. The sound of the wood smacking together filled the small arena. He watched Ember with great interest, trying to get a read of the woman.

No doubt she was beautiful. Raven hair down the middle of her back, porcelain skin and those striking violet eyes ... she was unforgettable. But there was something beneath her surface that seemed to draw Liam closer to her but he couldn't pinpoint what.

A chill ran down his spine as the duo continued their combat. She could fight like no one he had ever seen. Suddenly he knew why General Blanchard ordered his team to work with Amethyst.

Liam swallowed the hard lump forming in his throat. She was strong, fierce ... and deadly. One thing for certain was that Ember, and the three other members of Amethyst, were dangerous. Failure to keep that in mind could cost him and everyone on the planet their lives. Every member of Amethyst deserved respect for their abilities but they should also be feared.

He watched as Ember disarmed her teammate with extreme precision. She was different. Assertive. Confident. Sexy.

Deadly.

CHAPTER THREE

Lewis knocked Ember into the wall of her quarters. Picture frames rattled as his mouth covered hers. She tugged on his bottom lip with her teeth, pulling his shirt free from his pants. His tongue traced her lip before plunging deep into her mouth.

Ember ripped his shirt open and discarded the scraps. A mirror on the wall shattered from one of her shoes when she hastily kicked it off. Lewis impatiently tore at her shirt. He bit her shoulder as her bra came off. He picked her up as they kissed, knocking items off her dresser. Her nails clawed his shoulders as he unbuttoned her pants. Ember shoved him off and removed her clothes. Lewis kicked his remaining garments off and they collided on her bed.

Afterward, Ember stared up at the ceiling as Lewis went into her private bathroom to clean up.

"It certainly has been a while," Lewis said when he came out.

"Don't talk," Ember ordered.

Lewis grinned as he pulled up his pants. "Same old Ember. No cuddles?"

Ember rolled her eyes as she reached for a clean shirt.

"Want cuddles? Go find a girlfriend. Want dirty, toe curling sex? Talk to me."

Lewis sighed and bent down to kiss her but she pulled back.

"You know the rules. No kissing after sex."

Lewis shook his head. "You're a real piece of work, Wilson."

"I don't do nice," she flatly said. "I don't do intimacy."

"Stasis hasn't thawed the ice princess."

"I resent that."

"Forgot how much you hate the word."

"Laura is the princess, not me."

"And you despise your sister so much, you even dyed your hair to avoid looking like her."

Ember's eyes flashed. "Goodnight," she sternly said.

***

A part of her hated the way she acted the moment Lewis left. So what if he wanted to kiss her? Was that really a bad thing?

Yes, she decided. She didn't want emotions and feelings to get confused with their occasional physical relationship. So much of her focus over the last couple of years had been on preparing for the Genesis Project.

Genesis. The brainchild of a scientist who lived more than a thousand years ago. Once, Earth used clones as a tool for mankind. That was before the population knew the existence of other worlds and races. Now there were five teams of genetically enhanced humans to protect Earth's people and resources.

Each team had something different to offer. Led by Lance Daniels, Aureus was a team of pilots, characterized by their bright yellow eyes. They were the best of the best when it came to battles fought in space. Vinidus, known for their unnatural emerald green eyes, were weapons specialists. They were led by Jacob Conner, whom she had known since childhood. Mark Hopkins led the pumpkin-eyed Luteus team of sharpshooters. The teal-eyed team of information specialists, Caeruleus, was led by Shawn Silvers.

And then there was Amethyst. They were a mix of it all. Each of them at the top of their game. They were highly respected and admired. Thinking about the personal sacrifice it took to become the elite team pissed her off. The anger and hatred rolled around in her belly, setting her teeth on edge. Ember wasn't always like this. She used to be happy and better tempered.

All she ever wanted was the approval of her father. General Blanchard was the reason she joined the Air Force. She wanted to be just like him. But the General always favored her younger sister, Laura, because she most resembled their late mother. She would've done anything just for a kind word from him. When he couldn't give one, she changed herself.

When the opportunity came up to be a part of Genesis, Ember jumped at it. She hoped by becoming better than human, she would finally earn her father's love. Instead, he shunned her for it. To him, the only piece of her mother she had left was gone when her eyes changed from baby blue to violet.

Ember decided she had had enough. She started going by her mother's surname of Wilson and rejected the General and his perfect other daughter. To her, all the family she had was Amethyst.

But Lewis was different. They went through the academy together and always had a strong connection. She wasn't interested in anything more, regardless of how often he tried to change the boundaries of their relationship.

She pushed everything away from her mind. It would be a hard couple of days to train the military team to even keep up with hers and she needed rest. She rummaged through the brass cabinet in her bathroom until she found a prescription bottle of sleeping pills. Ember popped two sleeping pills and downed the glass of water sitting on her night stand. She quickly dozed off.

***

The next morning, Ember grumbled as she received her schedule. After breakfast, she was supposed to report to General Blanchard. What a lovely way to start the day.

"Morning," she mumbled to her squad as she sat down with her food.

"Not a morning person?" Liam asked as he joined them.

Ember stared hard at him as the rest of his team joined the long table. Ross had to look away from her.

"No, Wilson isn't much of a morning person," Lewis said.

"Or an afternoon person," Nova chimed in.

"Or an evening person," Morris added.

"Haha," Ember dryly said.

"Would've thought you'd be nice and relaxed after last night," Morris teased.

Ember narrowed her eyes. Lewis' ears turned pink.

"You are in for so much pain." Ice filled her voice.

"I'm sorry."

"Not yet, but you're going to be."

"I missed something," Liam said, looking confused.

"Don't worry about it," Lewis muttered.

Liam looked at Lewis and back at Ember. A part of him wanted to press further, but didn't want her to glare at him the way she was looking at her second-in-command. Whatever it was, it felt personal and it was best not to get involved. He just wanted to do his job and go back home, assuming there was one to go back to.

"Do you have a meeting with General Blanchard as well?" Liam asked, trying to break the tension.

Ember pursed her lips together and nodded.

"Great. I'll walk with you."

She didn't say anything as she stood up and walked off.

"You'd better go," Lewis muttered.

"Ember! Wait up!" Liam yelled.

When she didn't stop, he caught up to her in the hallway and grabbed her arm.

"What the hell?" Ember snapped.

"What's your problem with me?"

She grabbed his wrist and pulled it backwards. He bit his lip to keep from whimpering once she let go.

"I don't like being touched," she said before walking away.

"So noted." Liam rubbed his wrist. "Unless it's by someone under your command, right?"

Ember stopped in mid-stride. She turned on her heels, grabbed the back of his elbow, wrenching his arm against his back as her right hand pressed down against his shoulder. The Major winced as she kept the hold.

"Don't pretend you know me, Major Ross. Next time you want to talk about my personal life, I'll separate your shoulder from the socket."

"Okay." He swallowed.

"Glad we understand each other." She let go of her hold.

This time when Ember walked off, Liam kept up the pace slightly behind her.

Chapter Four

"Ah, good," the General said as they entered his office.

"You wanted to see us?" Ember questioned as she took a seat.

"I did. I wanted to let you both know I'm ordering a series of training exercises beginning at eleven hundred hours."

"Is that really necessary?"

"Yes, Ember, it is. Your teams need to work as a unit if we have any chance of success."

"Tell your boy to stay out of my way and follow orders, and everything will be fine."

"Now, hang on -" Liam interjected but she cut him off.

"I've seen your team in action and I wasn't impressed," she hissed. "It'll be better for everyone if you just acted as the backup my squad doesn't need."

"One simulation means nothing. We weren't prepared -"

"It was a test of your squad's mettle and you failed."

"Enough!" General Blanchard banged his fist on the desk. "Like it or not, this is the mission. There is more on the line than foolish pride. I won't let Earth be in jeopardy over your petty squabbles."

To Liam's surprise, Ember lowered her eyes.

"Good." Blanchard curtly nodded. "You two will be a cohesive unit. From this point on, you will be joined at the hip. You'll eat together, train together, even room together."

"Sir!" They protested in unison.

"If one of you has an itch, I expect the other to scratch it."

Ember and Liam turned and glared at one another but neither argued.

"Glad we had this talk."

General Blanchard rose from his desk and input a series of commands from his console. A holographic image appeared of a woman with long dirty blonde hair, light blue eyes, and a pretty, heart-shaped face.

"Do you know who this woman is?" Blanchard asked.

"Yes." Ember cleared her throat. She knew the woman well. There was a statue of her outside headquarters in West Virginia. Scientists had to take a master class on her in order to get their doctorate. "Doctor Madison Brooks."

"That's right. You have her to thank for the Genesis Project."

"Among other things. She was the savior of Earth over a thousand years ago," Liam chimed in.

"She was the face of the new world. At that point in our history, Earth's population had no knowledge of other worlds and alien races. Dr. Brooks was the one who explained the situation to the planet when a vengeful species known as the Synth were attempting to conquer," Ember stated. "The Intergalactic Security Commission was no longer a secret. That's when the world's military branches united under the Air Force."

"Hard to believe Dr. Brooks was a clone," Liam commented.

"Exactly. Clone or not, she and her counterpart, Mackenzie Rhodes, were our planet's most gifted minds in the last millennia." Blanchard nodded.

"Sir, what does Dr. Brooks have to do with us?" Liam asked.

"She was brilliant beyond the technological resources of her time. Like Genesis, she had designed a defensive program which couldn't be implemented until the discovery of sampsite long after her death."

"What kind of defensive system?" Ember asked.

"It was designed to find and neutralize any element or substance not natural to Earth," the General explained.

"Sounds dangerous," Liam said.

Ember rolled her eyes. "I assume the system is programmable to particular elements."

"Yes." General Blanchard nodded. "All that is needed is a small sample."

"Let me guess." Ember placed her feet on the General's desk. "Rudo's weather system uses something not organic to this planet."

"We've discovered croceus is the power source."

"So we just need to use this system to target the croceus and destroy the weather machine," Liam said.

"It's not that simple, you twit," Ember snapped. "We don't exactly have an abundance of croceus around."

"What's the big deal? We'll go get some."

"Croceus is found on PK-5873. The Maulians that inhabit the planet aren't exactly the friendliest bunch," General Blanchard said.

"Let my team go." Ember cut her eyes at Liam. "We can be in and out before the Maulians know we are there."

"Joined at the hip." The General enunciated each word. "You're not going anywhere without Major Ross."

"His team will just complicate things."

"Then you'd better start training together to learn how to work."

"This is ridiculous," Ember muttered under her breath.

The General walked around the desk, knocked her feet off, and bent down to get in her face.

"I don't care," he said in a low voice. "You will do as you are told or you'll go back in the hibernation chamber. And this time, I'll authorize behavior modification protocols. You'll wake singing every Disney song and having a strong urge to knit. Do I make myself clear?"

Ember glared in response to his threat but didn't argue. After a moment, he backed off and straightened his jacket.

"Dismissed."

***

A large portion of the afternoon was spent with both teams arguing. The Air Force unit wanted to show up Amethyst. The quartet viewed the others as a nuisance.

The General ordered the two leaders to share quarters. Being in close proximity to each other set both of them on edge. Neither trusted the other and resented the forced arrangements.

"I'm not at all bad," Liam told her as she made her bed.

"I'm sure you're not."

"Can't we ... why can't we get along?"

"Get along?" Ember stopped at the foot of the bed.

"Make the best of this situation."

"Let me spell it out for you." She sat down and placed her hands on her knees. "My goal here is to kill Rudo and save our planet by any means necessary."

"And I'm what's necessary."

"I doubt that."

"Why?"

"You're just a pretty boy with a gun. I've seen and trusted my fair share of good-looking guys who think they're something, and they always end up dead. This is dangerous. I want to get out of this with as few fatalities as possible."

"I do, too. We're on the same page. I am not your enemy."

"I know," she murmured.

The softness in her voice temporarily stunned him.

"You're not my enemy," she continued. "In a previous life, we might have been friends. That doesn't mean I want you around."

"Previous life?"

"I wasn't always like this," she explained, her voice gentle and velvet smooth. "I used to be warm and open. Back when I had blonde hair and baby blue eyes. I used to ..." she trailed off, her voice cracking slightly. "It was a different time."

"Ember, what the hell happened to you?"

Liam sat across from her on his bed, resisting the impulse to reach over and take her hands in his. Something in her eyes shifted from gentle to harsh.

"Don't get all touchy-feely on me. This isn't sharing hour. You serve as much usefulness to me as a Slinky. You're not really good for anything, but it would bring a smile to my face if I could push you down a flight of stairs."

"Ember, who lit the fuse on your tampon?"

"Be lucky you don't have any balls for me to kick you in."

Liam leaned forward slightly, peering at her.

"What?" Ember asked.

"I'm just wondering how you style your hair so the horns don't show."

Ember flashed him a humorless smile. "Original. I'm not a bitch."

"Seriously?" Liam made a face. "Could've fooled me."

"I'm blunt and honest."

"I love how you don't think it's the same thing."

She scoffed as she rolled backwards and laid down on the bed. Liam looked at her as she stared up at the ceiling and sighed.

"Look, I'm sorry," Liam muttered.

"Don't be. You're right. I've done nothing but antagonize you since we met."

"Is it going to stop?"

She shrugged. "Maybe."

He fell silent as he tried to sum up how he felt.

"I'm the new kid on your block. I'm just trying to understand and keep up."

His words struck a chord with her. She could relate to it all too well.

"All right."

"General Blanchard is right, Ember. We do need to work together if this mission is going to work."

"I agree."

Liam stood beside her bed and extended his hand. After a moment, Ember sat up and shook it.

"Ember Wilson," she politely said.

"Liam Ross. I look forward to working with you."

***

It surprised both teams when Ember and Liam appeared as a united front during the morning training.

"Is this a trick?" Lewis asked.

"Wilson is acting ... pleasant?" Nova questioned, chewing on gum loudly.

"Maybe General Blanchard drugged her," Morris speculated.

"Ooh, or he reprogrammed her somehow," Nova suggested.

"Very funny, boys," Ember said.

"Has the cat been somehow declawed?" Lewis asked.

In response, Ember punched him in the stomach. The second-in-command groaned as he took to one knee and held his abdomen.

"What's the matter, Lewis? Thought I'd lost my bite?"

"Sorry," he said, wheezing slightly.

As he caught his breath, Ember turned attention to the squad.

"From this point forward, there will be no more arguing, no petty competitions. We need to work together as a team if we have any hope of being successful."

One of the members of Liam's team raised his hand sheepishly. Ember gave a quick glance to his name tag before addressing him.

"No need to raise your hand, Lassiter. We're not in grade school."

"Sorry." He turned red. "Um, who do we report to?"

"Me." Liam and Ember said in unison. "No, I'm the leader."

"Oh, this is going to be good." Lewis rocked back on his heels, grinning.

"Knew it couldn't last," Nova muttered before blowing a bubble and popping it.

Ember and Liam looked at each other scornfully.

"General Blanchard put me in charge," he insisted.

"Frankly, I don't give a shit what the General said. My team will not be reporting to you."

"Ember, we talked about this," Liam emphatically said. "We need to unite-"

"Exactly, so why are you fighting me on this?"

"Genera Blanchard-"

"Told you to work with me to take down Rudo. I'm the one who knows how Rudo operates. I know the machine and the methods we're fighting against. You lack the skills and the knowledge necessary to lead us."

She poked him several times in the chest as she spoke. For a moment, he was taken aback by the passion in her voice. She wasn't speaking out of pride or anger. She felt she was right.

"I don't want any of our people to die," she said.

"Neither do I," Liam relented.

She studied him for a moment, her brow furrowing.

"How about this? We'll work as a tandem. We'll make decisions together."

"A compromise?"

Ember nodded. "For the mission."

She extended her hand and Liam didn't hesitate to shake it.

It wasn't the first time they had touched, but this time the moment their hands met, Liam felt a surge of energy coursing through his veins. The look in Ember's eyes said she felt it as well.

"We've reached an accord." Ember turned back to the team. "Report to who you feel most comfortable with."

***

Liam clapped his hands together and announced training would begin. The three Amethyst men looked at each other, amazed Ember was letting the Air Force Major take the lead. After a gentle nudging from her, they complied. If she was going to go along with it, so could they.

They spent the day on weapons training and cardiovascular conditioning. Ember taught the military personnel on a new blaster rifle they were testing out. Liam ran them through an obstacle course.

By the end of the day, Ember felt better about their odds. Liam Ross earned a little more respect in her eyes. They even sat down as a team for the evening meal.

"You would think since we're the saviors of the planet, we would get a better meal," Morris joked.

"Be glad it's not food pellets," one of Liam's men, Johnston, said.

"I'm surprised it's not. There's not an abundance of fresh food around these days," Nova said, a wad of gum in the corner of his mouth.

"Speaking of, I've been meaning to ask. How did you manage to find gum anyways?" Morris asked. "It's not exactly in abundance right now."

"I'm special." Nova grinned, the gum clinched in his teeth before sucking it back in.

"The General won't eat anything synthesized," Ember explained. "It may be bland, but it's food. Call it a perk for being on his station."

Liam leaned back in his chair and smiled as he watched everyone interact. Even Ember seemed to be in a good mood as she ate.

He wished they had gotten off on a better foot. Admittedly, he liked her. It was becoming easier to see past her tough exterior to see how beautiful she truly was.

"You're not so scary when you smile," Walsh commented, breaking into Liam's thoughts. At least he wasn't the only one who thought so.

"I'm scary?" Ember asked.

"Frightening is more like it," McKnight remarked.

Ember roared with laughter. Tears started rolling down her cheeks as she slapped the table.

"There you go being all scary again."

"Nah, Walsh, Wilson isn't scary. You just have to know how to deal with her," Lewis said.

"Oh, and I suppose you know how?" She raised an eyebrow.

"If those scratch marks are any proof, I'd say no." Nova laughed.

"Shows what you know. She likes it rough." Lewis playfully jabbed him.

"Not always."

The tone in Ember's voice caught everyone off guard. A curtain of black hair fell in her face as she looked down at her plate.

"What was that?" Lewis questioned.

"Forget about it."

She shifted uncomfortably in her chair as Lewis' purple eyes bore into her. Ember composed herself, looking up into his face.

"Sometimes I need more, but not from you." She smirked.

"Sounds like someone can't get the job done." Morris clamped his hand on Lewis' shoulder.

"Cut it out." Lewis shrugged him off.

The men howled with laughter as Lewis flushed.

"Cute, Wilson. Real cute."

Ember flashed him a grin, tossing back her hair.

***

Once everyone had their assignments, Michael Lewis visited Ember in her quarters. He was trying to sneak out quietly when Liam caught up with him in the hallway.

"Sorry," Lewis apologized as they bumped shoulders.

"It's no problem. What are you doing here?"

"Oh, um, nothing," Lewis muttered, rubbing the back of his neck.

Liam looked at him unconvinced. "Right. I'm just heading back to my room after a workout."

Lewis grinned. "Me too. See you later."

Liam's eyes narrowed as the other man brushed past him, whistling a happy tune.

Ember was sitting on her bed when Liam came in. He paused as he watched her rest her head against her knees and hug her legs to her chest.

"Are you okay?"

"Yes, I'm fine." Her voice was barely above a whisper.

His father always told him whenever a woman said she was fine, it usually meant she wasn't. He flung his towel down in the clothes basket and sat down next to her on the bed. He had expected her to snap at him or move away, but she rested her head against his shoulder instead.

"I'm not going to ask you what's wrong or encourage you to talk."

She lifted her head and peered up at him. A cloud of emotions rolled through her beautiful violet eyes.

"Do you consider yourself a whole person?"

Her question surprised him. "Yes, I do."

"I don't. I've been searching for something to fill the void."

"Is that why there's this thing between you and Lewis?"

"Excuse you?"

"I'm sorry, that didn't come out right."

"Something you want to ask me?"

Liam rubbed the back of his neck. "It's not my place to question."

"It's too late now."

"I've just wondered why you would sleep with someone under your command."

"Michael wasn't always under my command. We came up together in the academy. We ... go back a long ways. Sometimes it's just comforting to have a link to the past and to have a bond with someone like that."

"But you're not in love with him?"

"No. Sometimes I wish I was. Maybe I wouldn't feel incomplete if I did."

Not knowing what else to say, Liam wrapped an arm around her shoulders and pressed her closer to him. She let out a snort and leaped off the bed.

"Don't touch me." She nearly growled at him.

"I'm sorry. I didn't mean any harm." Liam looked bewildered at her.

"Just don't. I don't show weakness."

"Ember, I could never see you as weak."

She planned on snapping at him, but the look on his face said he was being serious.

"I admire you. Ember, you show strength beyond your given abilities."

"Don't patronize me."

"I'm not."

Liam pushed off the bed and walked over to her. He gripped her shoulders as they locked eyes.

"I can look in your eyes and see your strength and the pain behind it. Being open to me is not a weakness. We have to rely on each other for survival. I don't pretend to understand it, but I can see you've been through hell."

"That's putting it mildly." She swallowed hard. "You talk as if you care."

He lightly brushed a stray black hair from her pale face. "I do."

Ember looked confused by his tenderness. "Why?"

"Because you are so much more than the anger which seems to fuel you. Ember, you are special."

"My specialness came from a lab."

"No. It comes from here." He carefully placed a hand over her heart.

The simple act stunned her. For several quiet moments, she could only stare. The sincere look in his brown eyes took her breath away. She had to break his gaze, feeling completely uncomfortable and blindsided. Her face turned red as she excused herself and ran out of the room.

CHAPTER FIVE

As soon as the door slammed shut behind Ember, Liam felt like kicking himself. He didn't know what possessed him to express himself in that manner, but he was sure he frightened her. Ember would never let him close to her again.

To help clear his mind, he decided on another workout. Apparently Ember had the same idea. She was hitting a punching bag in the corner when he came in. It didn't go unnoticed when she started attacking the bag harder.

He grabbed a few hundred pound weights and put it on a weight lifting bar.

"You trying to impress me with a two-hundred pound bench?" Her voice echoed in the small room.

"Somehow I doubt there's anything I can do in here to impress you."

Ember shot him an icy glare and punched the bag again. Liam sighed and approached her.

"Look, I'm sorry if I somehow overstepped my boundaries."

Ember hit the bag hard enough it knocked into him. He steadied the bag and took a step back.

"Clearly I had a strong effect on you."

The force of the next blow broke the chain. The bag slammed against the wall, sand pouring out of a hole in the middle. His mouth fell open as he stared at the mess on the floor. Her ponytail whipped around, hitting him in the face as she turned on her heels and walked out.

As soon as the door shut behind her, Ember leaned against it as she struggled to regain her composure.

How did he get under her skin? Somehow he had gotten through her defenses. She had started to care about him more than she was comfortable with. The whole situation with him was unsettling. Liam Ross was certainly attractive. She had grown accustomed to men giving her attention based on her looks, but there was something else behind his expression. It was unfathomable to her.

Sweat dripped into her eyes, mixing with the tears she didn't know she had cried. When she went through the training necessary for the Genesis Project, she locked her heart away. Emotions would only get in the way. None of it seemed to matter when he looked into her eyes.

**

Ember was already in bed with her back to him when Liam returned. He felt relieved. He wasn't sure what to say, so it was better she was already asleep. He quietly crept in his bed and drifted off in minutes.

When he awoke the next morning, Ember was gone. He expected to see her in the mess hall but she didn't join the team for breakfast.

"Wilson said to tell you she would join you for the strategy meeting," Lewis informed him.

"Where is she?"

"Probably in the training center." Lewis shrugged.

"You didn't ask?" Liam raised an eyebrow.

"Hey, with Ember, sometimes it's best to give her time and space."

"General Blanchard said we're supposed to be-"

"Yeah, you repeating Blanchard's commands isn't going to win her over."

"I noticed. What's the deal between them? Aren't they family?"

"Blood doesn't make you family," Nova said. "If she wanted you to know, she'd tell you."

Morris studied Liam for a moment before chuckling and shaking his head.

"What?"

"Just strikes me funny as someone with the last name Ross trying to figure out a monster."

"Nah, Wilson isn't a monster. Although she when she's on the war path, it's best to stay out of her way." Nova elbowed Morris before stealing a potato from his plate.

"I know she's ... hey! Quit stealing my food."

"Got to be quicker than that, bud."

Liam frowned into his cup of instant coffee. Just when he felt like he was getting closer to her, something always showed him how wrong he was.

He couldn't wait to meet up with her to strategize their attack. When he entered, Ember was looking at a holographic projection of PK-5873.

"You're late." She didn't glance in his direction.

"Sorry," he mumbled.

"Most of the planet is rough terrain." She hit a few buttons on the console beneath the graphic. A section of the planet became highlighted and magnified. "This area has the highest concentration of croceus in these caves."

"I see. How do we mine it?"

"Carefully and with lasers. We can cut the crystal without damaging the cave."

"Crystal? I thought this was a mineral we were after."

"It's grown in crystalline form then crushed to be used."

"Oh." Liam felt sheepish.

"The hard part will be dealing with the Maulians." She frowned. "They don't understand our language and I doubt a translator droid will be effective."

"General Blanchard said they weren't friendly."

"He's right." Ember punched in a few commands and the projection of the brown planet was replaced by a bug like creature. It had short, stubby arms and legs, a round body, and massive wings. "What this world lacks in technology is made up for in brutality. They use spears for weapons, but I've seen them tear a grown man apart with their teeth."

"Their teeth?"

Ember shuddered. "A gruesome way to die."

"Surely a species so primitive couldn't be a match for our blasters."

"Let's hope it doesn't come to that. I would prefer no loss of life from any side."

"I agree."

"The Maulians are nocturnal so my suggestion is to approach during the day. Keep the ship above orbit and beam down, cut the sample, and get out. No muss, no fuss."

"Reasonable plan."

"The croceus is deep in the cave. Caution is strongly advised. If there's trouble, we may not be able to beam out until we reach the surface."

"Sounds simple enough. Why don't you let my team handle it? There's no sense in all ten of us going."

"We're one team now, remember? Besides, you'll need us if something goes wrong."

Liam snorted. "You just don't think we're up to the task."

"Now who's got an ego?" She turned to him. "Liam, that's not what I said."

"Say it. Tell me you think my guys are just as capable as yours."

She stared at him agape. "Where is this coming from?"

"You can't do it. You think you're better than me."

"Liam, what's the matter with you?"

"You've been nothing but a bitch to me since you came out of hibernation. I've done nothing to you and you turn your nose up at me, keeping me at arm's length."

Ember looked stunned at his tirade. "Look, Liam-"

"Just." He paused, holding up his hand. "I don't want to hear it. I tried to be open and you shut me out at every possible opportunity. Just you wait, Wilson. You'll see."

He left her standing with her jaw hanging open when he rushed out of the room.

***

"What do you think he meant by that?" Lewis asked when Ember told Amethyst what happened.

"I wish I knew." Ember sighed.

"He pulled a Wilson." Morris chuckled.

"What was that?"

"You know ... how you can get fired up and go off then just walk out of the room."

"Ah." Ember bit her lip. She did have a penchant for theatrics. "I'm sorry, guys."

"Hey, we've all seen each other at our best and worst."

"I think he has a crush on you, Wilson," Nova said.

"Now isn't the time for feelings. This is war."

Nova and Morris exchanged curious looks. "That's not what we expected you to say."

"What?"

"You know, something along the lines of you have no interest in him."

"Guys, what's the big deal?" Ember questioned.

"The big deal is you didn't automatically shoot the notion down."

Ember looked at them confused. The three men looked eagerly at her for a response.

"What do you want me to say?" she asked.

"Ember, do you have feelings for Ross?" Lewis asked.

"What? No, of course not." She shook her head. Ember rubbed her temple and forehead. "Maybe? I don't know. No, absolutely not."

"Is it your final answer?" Morris grinned.

"Shut up."

"Wow, Ember does have a crush."

"Shut up, Bryan." Ember elbowed him.

Lewis looked down at his plate, feeling his stomach churn. He knew Ember didn't share his feelings, but it didn't stop him from wishing she would change her mind.

Seeing the look on his face, Ember reached across the table to touch his hand. "Oh, Michael ..."

He pulled away from her, getting up from the table. "It's okay, Ember. I had no delusions about us."

He nearly knocked over one of the station's crew members who had approached them.

"What is it, airman?" Ember asked.

"Major Ross and his team are gone," he informed her.

"Gone?" Ember bolted upright. "What do you mean they're gone?"

"Major Ross said the General gave him permission to lead his team to PK-5873."

"Please tell me you're joking," Ember sternly said.

"No, ma'am. But I checked with General Blanchard who said to report to you."

"Thank you, airman," she said, dismissing him.

"What a moron!" Lewis exclaimed.

"Does he think he has something to prove?" Nova asked.

"Yes." Ember frowned. "And it's going to get him and his crew killed."

Chapter Six

Ember ordered Nova to ready their ship. They would be leaving as soon as he gave the word. Ember and Lewis headed to the armory to gather supplies while Morris went to tell the General they were heading after the wayward team.

"So, you really care about this guy?" Lewis asked as they packed charges for their blasters.

"I don't know. Don't ask me questions like that as we prepare for a rescue mission."

"You really think they are in trouble?"

"I think he acted brash and put his team at risk, yes."

Ember filled a bag with a laser cutter, night-vision goggles, a large first aid kit and rope. She threw in an illumination stick and extra charge packs before zipping up her green canvas bag.

"Nova is ready," Morris informed them.

Lewis tossed him a supply bag and Ember strapped a knife to her right ankle.

"Can never be too careful," she said when Lewis raised an eyebrow at her.

The three of them grabbed their black uniform jackets and headed to their ship.

"We have clearance," Nova told her as they boarded.

"Get us up in the air."

"Wilson, come in." The General's voice crackled over the intercom.

"I read you."

"Be safe out there and bring those men home."

"That is the plan, General."

"You know how dangerous the Maulians are. Watch each other's backs out there."

"Understood. Wilson out." She turned her attention over to Nova as he was putting in the planet coordinates in the ships navicomputer. "Go ahead and set us out for mark ten."

His purple eyes widened as he turned to her. "Mark ten? Wilson, safety recommendations for this vessel-"

"Mark eight, I know. It'll be okay."

"So you say."

"Nova, it's worth the risk if it means getting to the planet faster."

"Yeah, but in how many pieces?"

"What are you whining for? It's a recommendation, Nova. Not a law. This ship can do up to mark twelve before the hull begins to heat up."

"Fine. You're the boss," he grumbled but still complied.

They arrived to PK-5873 in record time. Ember's eyes narrowed when Nova dropped them out of light speed near the planet. At least Liam listened and kept his ship above the alien world's orbit.

"Keep us above orbit and use your comm to lock onto the computer. I want us to be ready to transport at any time," Ember ordered.

"Aye," Nova acknowledged.

Morris connected with the military vessel and pulled the transporter records from the computer log. The quartet beamed down to the planet's surface using the coordinates as a guide.

Unfortunately, they were under the cover of night. The moon reflected very little light so Amethyst activated their night vision goggles and moved cautiously.

Lewis picked up on human footprints leading to a cave which appeared to have been caved in and someone had dug out from inside.

"Looks like they were here," Morris commented.

"But where did they go?" Nova asked.

Ember peered into the mouth of the cave. The smell of blood and rotted flesh twisted her stomach. She emptied her stomach contents as she saw body parts scattered on the dirt floor.

"Ember?" Lewis looked concerned at her. It was unlike her to vomit while on a mission.

"I'm okay." She closed her eyes as she leaned against the stone, wiping her mouth clean. "We'd better move."

If the Air Force team fell under attack in the mine, they wouldn't be able to transport out. Signs the Maulians discovered them gave little hope of finding any other humans on the planet.

If Liam had managed to survive, he would've transported back to his ship. She looked at her men who agreed with her unspoken thought.

"We should've scanned for life signs before leaving our ship." Ember looked back at the cave and shook her head.

"Might not have done us any good. If they were still trapped in here and alive, our sensors wouldn't have been able to penetrate the mine," Morris told her.

"Right."

"Let's get out of here before we're dessert," Lewis softly said, touching her arm.

"I'm really sorry, Ember." Nova gave her hand a gentle squeeze. Sadness filled her heart as she nodded.

The group gathered together to activate their beacon when they heard shouts for help. Ember darted off without hesitation with the others close on her heels. As they ran, they pulled out their blasters.

A large group of Maulians surrounded the entrance to another mine. Ember fired the first shot into the back of the largest winged enemy. It let out a high pitched scream as it fell to the ground. The others turned their attention to Amethyst, baring their teeth and shaking their spears over their heads.

"Get them away from the cave!" Ember yelled to Lewis and Morris.

They nodded. "Come on, you oversized moth! Let's see what you can do," Lewis taunted.

"Why did I leave my fly swatter at home?" Morris joked as he opened fire.

A spear whizzed by Ember's head as she opened fire. Red blaster fire from Nova ricochet off the entrance to the cave, killing a Maulian who was attacking Henry Lassister. Out of the corner of her eye, she saw a mangled body just outside the mouth of the mine. Two of the creatures flew to her side, clawing for her face. She quickly covered her face before dodging to the side and shooting her attacker. Apparently she wasn't quick enough as purple blood started to drip from a cut on her cheek. A human scream drew the attention of others. The smell of blood filled the air and the cries stopped. Morris and Lewis managed to cut down the numbers at the cave and the captives ran. Left behind was the shredded remains of flesh and blue material.

"Pull back!" Ember ordered.

She caught a glimpse of two more Air Force uniforms past her as the captives escaped. A spear aiming for Morris became lodged in the stone of the mine. A Maulian tried to bite the tech guru. Instead, Nova shot it in the back. Amethyst regrouped, cutting down the rest of the world's inhabitants when they attempted to swarm.

"Is everyone all right?" Ember asked, wiping a trickle of blood from a cut she had on her chin.

Liam and two other men joined them, covered in dirt and blood. Morris was cradling his arm after being scratched but no one appeared to have been bitten.

"We're okay now," Liam said.

"Is this all?" Lewis inquired.

Liam nodded. "It ... it was terrible."

"Let's talk on the ship." Ember motioned for everyone to gather around.

A bright light enveloped them as another swarm of Maulians spotted them. Since the Maulians had no form of space travel, the team began to relax. Lewis checked over Morris and Ember ordered the Air Force team to sit down to be checked over.

"What happened?" Ember asked as she evaluated Henry Lassister's wounds.

"We went in deep to mine the crystal." Lassiter winced as she began cleaning the cuts on his face and neck. "We heard a loud screech and we were swarmed before we knew what was going on."

Ember frowned as she continued the medical evaluation. Lassiter seemed to be the worst. His protective armor kept him from losing his right arm but he did have two fingers missing. Judging by the wheeze in his voice, he had at least one broken rib if not more. She pulled a medical scanner from her kit and stopped his bleeding.

"Didn't you have a look out?" Lewis asked.

"We did," Johnston spoke up. "Walsh. No one has seen him."

The body parts at the front of the mine. Ember swallowed, trying to shove the image from her mind. She turned her attention to Corey Johnston, using the scanner to stop the blood from dripping out of a deep gash on his neck.

"You'll both need to head to the medical bay once we get back to the station but you'll be okay."

She went to check on Liam but he waved her off.

"I'm okay."

"You're bleeding."

"So are you. At least, I assume this is blood. Do you literally bleed purple?"

"The genetic manipulation from Genesis changes the molecular structure of DNA, skin cells, and yes, even the color of blood. It's how our eyes are affected as well," she explained. "Hey, don't change the subject."

He sighed. "It's just a scratch, Ember."

"And scratches from the Maulians can get infected. Don't be a baby."

Liam glared at her but relented. He presented her with his hands and neck which had little marks on it.

"Morris is good to go," Lewis informed her.

"Are you?" She looked at him as she worked over Liam's cuts.

"I'm fine," he assured her.

"See? Nothing to it," she said once she finished tending to Liam.

"Are we good to take off?" Nova asked.

"Yes but who is going to pilot the other ship?"

"I will." Lewis volunteered.

"You sure?"

"No sweat." He flashed a grin and transported over.

Morris helped get Lassiter and Johnston into medical beds. Nova pulled away from the planet, going a safe distance before activating the hyper drive.

"Are you okay? You were bleeding from your cheek and chin earlier." Liam lightly touched her face.

"One of the benefits to Genesis is having super-fast healing powers. I'm already healed." She jerked her head away from him. "Liam, what were you-"

"I wish I knew, Ember. Sorry doesn't cover it. I don't have a logical explanation..."

"You'd better think of one fast before you are in front of the General."

"I know, but we did get enough croceus to use. And I got this." He pulled a purple gem from his pocket and presented it to her.

Ember looked at him curiously as she accepted it. She rolled it around in her hand before holding it up to the light. It was a few centimeters long with perfect clarity and fit in the palm of her hand.

"You got this for me? Why?"

"The mine had a bunch of other crystals than the croceus. We were midway through the cave when I saw this. It... reminded me of you." He turned bright red at his admission.

She managed to keep from blushing as well. Instead, she pocketed the gem and nodded.

"Thank you."

"You're welcome."

***

"You put your men's lives in danger and you risked the rest of our mission." General Blanchard circled Liam.

The Air Force Major stood at full attention in the center of the General's office.

"Yes, sir."

"You could've been killed."

"Yes, sir."

"You disobeyed a direct order."

"Yes, sir."

"Several good men died due to your negligent behavior."

"Yes, sir."

"I should have your stripes for it."

"Yes, General."

"What do you have to say for yourself?"

"We completed the mission, sir."

"Yes, but at what cost? You lost three good men. If you were with Amethyst like you should've been, that might not have happened."

Liam's entire body went rigid as the General circled him again.

"Well, Major?"

"I felt my team was up to the task."

"There's a reason I told you to work with Amethyst."

"I understand, General."

"Do you?" Blanchard stood toe-to-toe with Liam. "Major, count your lucky stars I still need you or you would be in the brig. As it stands, there will be a hearing after Rudo has been stopped."

The door chimed several times before Blanchard growled as he took a step back from the Major.

"Come in!" He barked at the door.

Surprised rippled through both men when Ember stepped in.

"This is a private meeting, Ember."

"Yes, General, I understand that, but I feel like I should be here."

"Under what grounds?"

"Your orders, sir. Wherever Major Ross goes, I must follow."

Blanchard grinned, turning back to Liam.

"Even my wayward daughter can follow orders, Major Ross."

"I'd like to take full responsibility," Ember stated.

"What?" Both men looked at her in shock.

"I wasn't fair to Major Ross. I purposely kept him in the dark about my plans and refused to help get our teams prepared for the mission."

"General, that's not true," Liam protested.

"Quiet," Ember sharply said. "Sir, I created an environment which was toxic to everyone. Instead of coming together as one, my team alienated his. Because of my actions, Major Ross didn't feel like he could trust me. It's my fault and I'm ready to accept punishment."

"You would be willing to concede to me?" Blanchard questioned.

"Yes, sir. Even if it means I must go back in the stasis tube once our mission is over."

Ember's eyes shone brightly with intensity. Liam's jaw hung open, feeling completely stunned she was willing to fall on the sword for him. Blanchard ran a hand through his short graying hair, at a loss for a course of action. Ember shook her jet black hair free from her collar. Liam caught a glimpse of the purple gem he gave her fastened on a chain around her neck. She looked wavering in her resolve as the General stared her down.

"Major, you're free to go," Blanchard spoke after several moments.

"Sir?" Liam blinked.

"I know she doesn't think I do, but I know my daughter. For her to do what she just did showed impressive growth. Either she really wants to save you or she really thinks she was in the wrong. Either way, the fact she was willing to go back into stasis tells me everything I need to know. Now, both of you get out of my office."

***

"Thank you for what you did back there," Liam said once they were in their room.

"Are you insane?" Ember challenged.

"I'm sorry-"

"Sorry? Liam, you could've been killed!"

"I know!" He shouted back to her. His shoulders slumped as he dropped his tone. "I'm an idiot."

Ember shoved against his chest, grunting.

"You... could have.... When I saw the body parts in the mine, I thought..."

Liam looked at her stunned. This was a tough, highly skilled woman - a soldier - crying at the thought of losing him.

"You really are an idiot." She wiped her eyes.

Without a thought, Liam took her into his arms, kissing her passionately. She hesitated for a moment before wrapping her arms around his neck and returned his embrace. He gripped her tightly, almost afraid if he let go, she would disappear. Or worse, reject him. Instead, she pressed her body into his, thrusting her hands into his hair. Liam picked her up, accidentally slamming into her dresser. She pulled away as he bit down on her lower lip.

"No, not like that," she panted. "I just need you. Give me you, not what you think I want."

Ember pulled him close again, wrapping her legs around his waist. This time, he poured all his emotions into the kiss. He felt light-headed when she kissed him back with the same amount of intensity. She broke the embrace long enough to discard her shirt. She bent to kiss him again, but he stopped her.

"You are so beautiful," he said, stroking her cheek. "So beautiful."

The look in his eyes made her heart skip a beat. She bit her bottom lip, grinning. There was no stopping them when she reached for him again, the two becoming one on his bed.

***

It was new, waking up in someone's arms. New, yet welcoming. Cradled in Liam's arms, Ember listened to the gentle rhythm of his heart. He lightly ran a thumb up and down her shoulder. He still couldn't believe she was his.

"I don't want to move," she muttered against his chest.

"Who says you have to?"

"The alarm which will tell us to get back to work. I'm not ready to deal with the world outside this room." She looked up at him as he chuckled. "What's so funny?"

"I'm still in awe you're here."

"After three times last night, you're still surprised?" she teased. "You must not get a lot of action."

"Don't joke. I'm being serious." He rolled onto his side, looking deep into her purple eyes as he stroked her cheek. "You're incredible, Ember. I've wanted to be with you the moment we met but didn't dare dream you could ever want me."

"I do. I thought I lost you once. I don't plan on it a second time."

He touched the amethyst stone she still wore around her neck. His eyes twinkled as he bent to kiss her. Both groaned as the alarm went off.

"I wish I could put a blaster hole through the damned thing." She rolled out of bed.

"It wouldn't change a thing."

"Would make me feel better," she mumbled.

"So quick with your gun." Liam grinned, planting a quick kiss on her lips before getting dressed.

"Hey, you were grateful for it when you were nearly eaten by a bug."

"For the rest of my days."

She paused before fastening her belt. Something in the way he said it made her want to smile and bolt out the door at the same time.

"We should meet up with everyone."

"Ember." Liam grabbed her as she headed for the door. "Don't run from me. I don't mean to scare you."

"You? Frighten me?" She scoffed. "Hardly. But we do have a meeting to get to."

The rest of their team was already seated when they arrived for the debriefing with General Blanchard.

"Nice of you two to join us," Morris teased.

"Quiet." She snapped.

The General cleared his throat to grab everyone's attention.

"Thanks to the stupid antics of Major Ross, we have enough croceus to search for Rudo's weather machine."

"I think there was a compliment in there."

The General narrowed his eyes and ignored him.

"However, we have an issue. A big one."

"Of course." Ember rolled her eyes. "Now what?"

"Clayton has activated the machine. California is under ice." He paused while the news sunk in. "He calls it the Winter's Kiss."

"So we lost D.C. and the west coast," Ember said.

"Yes," the General confirmed. "In a matter of moments, too."

"So why can't we use our system to destroy his?" Nova asked.

"Because we're going to need his computer to reverse it," Morris explained.

"Precisely, but we can still use the croceus to locate him."

"What makes you think Rudo will be with the machine?" Lassiter inquired.

"He'll be there. He won't be able to resist," Ember said.

"Rudo is power-hungry and this is the source of his rise. He won't be able to help himself," Lewis stated.

"Have we located him yet?" Liam asked.

"We haven't turned on the machine yet to search. Thought you or Ember would like to throw the switch."

Ember managed to keep from grinning as she approached. A glass tube filled with the crushed yellow crystal sat on the table. She poured the powdered element in the cylinder. Liam stood beside her as the machine hummed to life. They held hands under the table so no one could see as Liam activated the search function. The computer lit up and after several moments, displayed a holographic projection for the room to see.

"It's an island off the coast of Scotland in the North Sea. It must be man-made. The computer doesn't have a record of its existence," Ember stated. "Then that's where we're going," Liam said. "How?" Lewis questioned. "We can't exactly fly in. And you know Rudo's defenses are going to be stronger than before."

"Who says we can't fly in?" Ember asked.

"It's an island. I think he would notice."

"Not after we dive." Ember grinned.

She enhanced the image of Scotland, focusing on the coastal city of Aberdeen.

"This is Scotland's largest port city. Major Ross and I can rent a boat and sail out to the island. Then it'll be a matter of disabling any defense shield and landing our ship."

"You talk as if it's a simple thing, Wilson."

"Any shielding will be weaker under water due to the sea life. It won't be a problem. Plus we have Morris who can scramble any security feed."

"I think you're leaving out a factor," Johnston spoke up. "As soon as we get close to our planet, we'll be under attack."

"That's true." Ember's lips pressed into a thin line. "We should take our fighters and try to land in the water near the city of Wick. It should be far enough away to avoid over-exposure."

"We should be able to regroup once we are on the surface to see if we can even land a fighter on the island," Liam spoke up.

"Right." Ember nodded.

"I would feel better about our chances if we could see the stronghold," Lewis commented.

"Maybe we can." Liam rubbed his chin in thought. "Morris, think you can manipulate a satellite since we know the location?"

"I should be able to." Morris approached the computer and set to work. After several minutes, the hologram was replaced by a live video feed. "Boo ya!"

Ember wasn't sure what she expected. Another security fortress like they encountered in Texas, perhaps. Instead, the camera showed them a dilapidated cabin surrounded by trees.

"That's it? Are you sure?" Johnston questioned.

"Positive." Morris sniffed. He didn't like someone questioning his skills.

"Don't be fooled by the meager appearance," Blanchard warned. "Rudo is crafty and well-versed in deceit."

"Or he could be over-confident," Lewis pointed out.

"Either way, we should be on guard," Liam said.

"Agreed. I still think diving is the best way to get in undetected," Ember said.

"I concur. You have four hours to get ready," Blanchard instructed.

***

"Using fishing boats, diving underwater, unsure if we can land our ship ... this is either going to be the greatest plan ever, or we're all going to die horribly and painfully," Nova joked as the team left the meeting. "I know." Ember's purple eyes danced gleefully. "What an adventure!"

The group separated to prepare to leave the station. Liam and Ember went back to their room to get their gear. She stopped suddenly in the doorway, causing Liam to collide into her.

"Ember, what the hell?"

"Why are you here?" Ember asked, ignoring Liam.

He peeked around her shoulder to see a blonde wearing a white sundress sitting on Ember's bed. Ember stepped to the center of the room, glaring at the young woman. The lady in white seemed to be unfazed by Ember's anger. She smoothed out her skirt, gracefully standing up and flashed a perfect smile.

"Well, hello to you, my dear sister," the other woman greeted, her voice sounding rich in a Southern accent. "Sister?" Liam questioned. "Laura, what are you doing here?" Ember inquired. "I'm just gonna ... leave you two alone." Liam slowly backed out of the door. "Who is this?" Laura asked, her baby blue eyes scanning him. "It's fine." Ember motioned for him to stand next to her. "Major Liam Ross, this is Laura Blanchard." Laura smiled again, showing off a row of perfect white teeth. "You're handsome." "He's mine," Ember snarled. "Answer my question." "Fine." Laura squared her shoulders back. "Daddy brought me on the station to protect me. He says you're getting ready to take on a dangerous mission." "All my missions are dangerous, princess." "Okay ..." the younger woman began fidgeting. "I just wanted to see you." "We haven't seen each other in years. Why now?" "Ember, you're my sister. I love you."

Ember snorted. "You want something, don't you?"

Laura's shoulders slumped as she chewed on her bottom lip.

"This isn't how I wanted our reunion to go."

"What did you expect, Laura? For me to cry and embrace you?"

"I don't know, Ember. Just wanted to say I love you and good luck."

With a heavy sigh, Laura turned to leave. Liam nudged Ember, nodding emphatically toward her sister. She sighed and gave his hand a squeeze.

"Laura, wait."

Laura paused at the door, slowly turning around. She crossed her arms over her chest and narrowed her eyes, obviously preparing for a fight.

"What?"

"You ... you're right. You're the only sister I have. Thank you for coming."

Ember struggled with her words. The two women stared at each other for several moments, not saying anything, until Laura smiled. She crossed the room quickly, throwing her arms around her older sister. Ember hesitated before returning the embrace. Laura sobbed into Ember's shoulder, clutching the other woman tightly.

"I love you, Ember. Always know that."

"I ... I know. I do, too."

Laura cried harder at her sister's admission. Ember couldn't handle the display of emotion, pushing the blonde gently away.

"Be safe, okay?" Laura wiped her tears away.

"Always." Ember managed a small smile.

"Call me when you get back. We'll do lunch."

Ember looked over at Liam who nodded at her.

"Okay."

Laura hugged her again before heading toward the door. She paused, tossing her long blonde hair behind her as she looked over her shoulder.

"I don't know what you've done to my sister, Major Ross, but thank you."

After Laura left, the couple fell silent. Ember was still uncomfortable by the emotional exchange with her sister, but ultimately was glad it happened.

"So," Liam broke the quiet. "I'm yours?"

"Yes. It's too bad if you have a problem with it."

Liam grinned, wrapping his arms around her. "I think I can handle it."

"Good. Lock the door and prove it to me."

***

The rest of the team looked at the couple crossly as they scurried into the equipment locker an hour later.

"We were getting ready to send out a search party," Lewis stated.

"No need." Ember ignored his curious gaze. "We only have a little time, so listen up. I won't be repeating myself."

She pulled four metal bands from the wall of weapons and handed two to Liam.

"These look like a normal comm cuff but are more enhanced than our usual ones. This will enable the ship to lock onto us and it can keep an eye on our vitals as well."

"So we'll be able to beam back if we run into trouble."

"Exactly, Lassiter. I want everyone to grab a pair."

She pulled two blasters from the wall. Unlike the standard weapon, these two had longer, skinner barrels and were lighter.

"Designed to work under water. The energy shots are more concentrated and less likely to dissipate. Plus we can fire faster."

"Nice," Liam whistled, holding up the gun for a closer inspection.

"Lewis, I want you to monitor my signal from the ship once we get in the water. I'll let you know if we need an evac."

"You got it."

"Nova, get the ship ready."

"Aye."

#

The team gathered their weapons and supplies. As they sat down together for a quick meal, Ember excused herself.

"You okay?" Liam asked, grabbing her arm as she passed.

"Something I need to take care of."

She didn't knock before entering General Blanchard's office. He looked at her for several moments before speaking. "Is your team ready?"

"They are in the mess now. We'll be heading out within the hour."

"Excellent."

The air became tense as the two stared at each other.

"Your sister was here."

"I know. I saw her."

He raised an eyebrow, trying his best to suppress his surprise over this news.

"Do you regret it?"

"I regret a great many things, Ember. You need to be more specific."

"Me. Do you regret me?"

"I do."

Her heart sank at her father's admission. She felt like kicking herself for opening herself up for the pain and disappointment only he could administer.

"But not in the way you think," the General continued, his voice cracking slightly. "I regret not listening to you when you tried to tell me about Rudo. I regret the way I handled you joining the Genesis Project. Our relationship as it currently stands eats at me. The fact you don't call me your father keeps me awake at night. Yes, I have many regrets. You being my daughter isn't one of them."

It was the first time he had looked into her purple eyes for any length of time since she joined Amethyst. He was opening himself up to her, and for the first time in years, Ember didn't feel like attacking him. Her bottom lip trembled slightly as she was taken aback by his sincerity.

"Say something, please," he implored.

She couldn't. She was afraid if she opened her mouth, she would burst into tears. Instead, she shoved him, causing him to fall into his desk. She spun around, forcing herself to regroup.

"I know you must be filled with hatred. I deserve your resentment. But, Ember, I am so proud of the woman you've become. I am proud to call myself your father. I love you. I always have."

Ember held her breath, trying to slow down her racing heart.

"Ember ..."

She shocked both herself and him when she whirled around and hugged him. It took him a moment to comprehend before returning her embrace. Tears flowed freely from her as she buried her face into his shoulder.

"I'm sorry."

"Oh, Ember," Blanchard gripped her tighter. "I'm the fool here, not you."

It wasn't complete forgiveness, but it was a start. He didn't stop her when she pulled away.

"I've got to go."

"Yes. You have a planet to save."

"Goodbye ... Dad."

The five-star General in Earth's only military cried like a baby the moment his daughter closed his office door behind her.

Chapter Seven

"Once we get close to Earth's orbit, everyone needs to be prepared for combat," Ember stated as the team left the space station.

Lassiter and Johnston flew in two small fighters flanking the empirical-class ship.

"I've got a bad feeling about this," Liam murmured. "Just strap in and hang on. This could get bumpy," Ember said.

"We've got incoming," Nova announced as they approached the   planet.
"Shields!"

"Evasive   maneuvers,"   Lewis   ordered.
"You think?" Nova snapped.

The sound of Nova popping his gum rang in her ear as the ship lurched. It shuddered and groaned when Nova rolled the ship to avoid blaster fire. Morris and Lewis unbuckled their belts and ran to the turrets on the ship.

"Don't be fancy. Just get us to the surface," Ember ordered.

Green blaster fire shot back at the red targeting them. The vessel creaked and shook, but the shields held. Tiny explosions lit up the blackness of space. The ship lurched as Nova maneuvered them through the fray. A loud bang hit the side of the ship. Ember gasped, holding on to the straps of her harness. The lights dimmed in the cockpit momentarily before going out completely.

"Hang on!" Sounds of Nova pounding on the console and his annoying gum popping echoed. A moment later, the electronic panel lit up and the seating area was bathed in a red light.

"Nova, what was that?"

"Sorry, Wilson. Seems we lost someone," Nova announced.

"And the shields are gone."

"Get us to the rendezvous point while we're still in one piece!"

"Working on it."

Ember unfastened her belt, ignoring Liam as he reached out for her in protest. She stood behind Nova, listening to the sound of the ship under attack. Nova's brow was furrowed, his lips pressed into a thin line as he concentrated.

"Break there." Ember pointed to the left.

The ploy to break through the blockade would've worked if one of the enemy fighters hadn't flown into the hull of the vessel. Sparks flew around them before plunging them into darkness. A moment later, a soft glow emitted from lights on the floor.

"Emergency power activated," a computer voice rang out. "Hull integrity has been compromised. Estimated time before breach is three minutes."

"That's our cue," Nova said, unbuckling his straps.

"Lewis, do you read?'

"We're already heading to the pods, Wilson."

The temperature started to rise as the trio ran to the shuttle bay. The alarm started blaring. A countdown started over the speakers. Each member managed to climb in the small escape pod before the shuttle bay started tearing apart. Ember watched helplessly from the small port hole in her pod. High above Earth's orbit, the ship broke apart before exploding. Bright light filled the area. Pieces of metal flew past her and broke up in Earth's atmosphere. She leaned back in her chair as the pod began to accelerate. A parachute deployed, slowing down her descent. The pods landed near each other, splashing down off the coast of Scotland. A tidal wave was created due to the force, causing them to float further away from land. Ember opened the hatch and crawled to sit on the opening. She watched as Liam pulled himself on top of his pod and immediately started throwing up. Around her, Lewis, Nova, and Morris sat on top of their pods. A cool ocean breeze blew in her face, the scent filling her nose. It felt great to breathe real air and not the sterilized oxygen created by Lunis Two.

Parts of her destroyed ship floated around the five pods. She saw one of their fighters land on a nearby aircraft carrier.

"Is everyone okay?" Lewis asked.

"Okay is a relative term." Liam touched the open gash on his cheek.

"We're okay, Wilson." Morris rolled his eyes at Liam.

A small boat from the carrier rescued them from the water and brought them to shore. Henry Lassiter joined them to regroup.

"I'm sorry. I tried to help Corey out ..."

"I know. We were overrun." Liam patted him on the shoulder.

A medic healed Lassiter's injured hand and Liam's cuts. A local fisherman named Duncan Mackenize persuaded them to join his family for dinner. Ember wanted to protest as they really should be making their way to the island, but decided to use the opportunity to see if he might have any useful information. Besides, everyone could use a little rest and food before proceeding to Rudo's hideaway.

"Fresh seafood! I haven't seen this in a long time." Nova plopped down in a chair.

"Mind your manners." Ember scolded.

"It's all right, dear." Duncan's wife, Arabella, smiled as she placed corn on the cob on the table. "He's a growing boy."

"He's no boy. He's thirty-four." Ember slapped Nova's wrist as he reached for a third piece of bread.

Nova stuck his tongue out at her as Mrs. Mackenzie gave him more bread.

"Are you going after the island?" Duncan asked.

"How did you know?" Liam questioned.

"A ship manages to break through the blockade and land with barely a scratch on its crew? Call it a lucky guess."

"How come your eyes are strange?" Duncan's daughter, Davina, inquired.

"Davina!" Arabella admonished.

"It's okay." Ember waved her hands. "I know we're unusual looking." She leaned in, keeping her eyes locked on Davina's. "Want to know a secret?" Davina's eyes widened as she nodded. "You can't tell anyone."

"I promise," Davina breathlessly said.

"All right." Ember motioned for the young girl to lean in and she complied. "We're actually superheroes."

Davina's eyes lit up. "Really?"

Ember nodded. "Have you heard about the man controlling the weather?"

She nodded. "He froze parts of America."

"That's right. We're the ones who are going to stop him."

Davina whistled. "You must really be a superhero."

"Except for Ross." Morris playfully ruffled Liam's hair.

Davina looked at Liam and back to Ember, raising an eyebrow and not looking too impressed with the Major.

"He's close," Ember assured her.

"You are vouching for me?"

"I suppose so." Ember winked.

The team enjoyed the meal, talking noisily amongst the Mackenzie family. Duncan motioned for Ember to join him outside as the others enjoyed dessert.

"So you're really going after the island."

"What do you know?"

"It appeared overnight. I took my boat over there."

His eyes looked grave as his voice dropped to a whisper.

"It's no ordinary island, lass. Don't trust your senses. Believe nothing you see."

"What happened?"

"There was no noise, yet birds flew at me. I got close to the cabin and was chased off by trees."

"Trees." Ember arched an eyebrow.

"Don't mock me or think of me as a fool, lassie. It's dangerous."

"I'm sorry. I don't mean to be rude."

"You better hope you truly are a superhero, lass, if you plan to make it out alive."

***

Duncan drove them into town and helped find the scuba equipment they needed. Since their ship was gone, they rented two boats and gear to pass themselves off as fishermen. Liam and Ember got into their wet suits as they prepared to leave.

"Good luck," Duncan said, handing her an oxygen helmet.

"Thank you for your kindness." Ember smiled as she shook his hand.

Liam grabbed her arm as the team loaded their equipment.

"I need to talk to you."

"Can it wait?"

"Please?"

She studied his pleading brown eyes for a moment and sighed.

"Fine, but this better be good."

They walked around a small shack for privacy.

"What is so important it couldn't wait until we got back?"

"We may not make it off the island -"

"Don't think like that."

"There's a possibility, Ember. Don't be dismissive."

"All right." She placed her hands on her hips. "Go on."

"I just wanted to say ... " His brow furrowed as he struggled for his next words. "You've been the biggest pain in my ass since the moment we met. You're abrasive, controlling, and probably the most difficult woman I've ever met. You've fought me every inch of the way and have challenged me in every possible way. God help me, woman, I love you." Liam wrapped his arms around her. "With all my heart, Ember. Every fiber of my being belongs to you."

Ember smiled and stroked his cheek. "I know."

Before Liam could respond, Ember kissed him and walked back to the boat.

"All right, gentlemen. This is what we've trained for. Lassiter and Lewis are with me in this boat. Nova and Morris will be with Ross. Morris, stay two klicks away. I don't want to arouse suspicion."

"You got it," Morris acknowledged.

"Everyone still good with the new plan? Any questions?"

"I got one." Nova raised his hand. "What do we do if we catch a fish?"

#

The cool breeze coming off the water felt inviting on her face as they stopped at the assigned coordinates. Ember tucked her jet black braid under her wetsuit and readied her air tank.

"Watch your back," Lewis told her as he handed her an oxygen helmet.
"You, too."

Lewis connected her tank and she looked over at Liam. He gave her a thumbs up and dove into the water. Once they had swum out several yards, Ember activated a feature on the bracelets to illuminate their surroundings.

Ember scanned the area and found a massive energy signature under the island. To her immense surprise, the only resistance they met while swimming to the spot was several schools of fish. On a coral reef sat the source of the energy. A bronze metallic machine with tons of buttons and lights of several colors lit up. On the lower right corner was a lever.

"What do you think this is?" Liam questioned, his voice rang through the communicator in the helmet.
"No clue. It's emitting a high energy signature. Maybe this is the shield?"
"I don't know, Ember. I've got a weird feeling about this."
"I do, too. Be on guard."

She pulled the lever down, but nothing happened. Even the hum from the machine stayed the same. She searched for a simple way to turn the machine off but there was no change regardless of how many buttons she pressed.

"What are you doing?" Liam watched as she pulled out her blaster.
"What do you think? I'm going to blow it up."
"Do you think that's a good idea? We're not sure what this thing is!"
"Relax. It'll be fine."

She fired several shots and it sparked before the lights went off. As soon as it did, the temperature in the water seemed to change from cold to lukewarm. A loud groan echoed around them but they couldn't tell where it came from.

"Uh,   oh."
"Ember, what did you do?"

The machine shook and creaked before breaking apart. Hundreds of mechanical piranha came out.

"Oh,   shit!"   Ember   exclaimed.
"Crap, crap, crap!" Liam kicked hard away from the machine.
"I think you mean trap!"

Ember fired her weapon but only destroyed a few of them. Liam grabbed her wrist and kicked for the surface. They kept firing their blasters but were becoming overwhelmed. Several of the robotic fish ate through her flippers before they were destroyed by Liam. Metal teeth snagged their suits, causing minor rips. Still, they swam as fast as they could.

Halfway to the surface, a piranha ate the connector to her air tank. Ember gasped and began to choke as air left her.

"Ember!"

The robotic fish started hitting her helmet, causing it to crack. Liam managed to stop the remaining piranha, but the damage had been done. Water quickly filled in, making breathing impossible. By the time he reached the sandy beach, Ember was unconscious. He couldn't get his helmet off fast enough.

"Don't die on me, Ember."

Water splattered as he removed what was left of her helmet but she remained motionless. He tilted her chin and pinched her nose, ignoring the insistent voice of Michael Lewis over the comm. He blew air into her mouth several times before giving her chest compressions.

"Come on!" He yelled before blowing into her mouth again.

Water rushed from her mouth as she began to cough.
"Ember."

She sat up, gasping for air. He pressed his forehead into hers as she started to breathe normally.

"Wilson, status." Lewis's voice crackled. "We ... are on the beach." "Roger."

She closed her eyes and exhaled deeply. She momentarily allowed herself to lean into Liam

"Are you okay?" he asked, kissing her temple. "Thanks to you." "Figured I owed you." She chuckled. "That's right. I guess we're even." "Don't make it a habit of scaring me." "No promises."

They got out of their scuba gear and discarded it.

"Should we wait on the others?" "No." Ember shook her head. "They will catch up. Let's scout ahead."

Duncan's earlier warning was still fresh in her mind. It might look like an ordinary island, but Rudo was skillful at deception. The hairs on the back of her neck stood on end and her sense of awareness heightened. The birds in the trees seemed to be hopping on different branches, keeping up with their speed. Even the smell was different from the mainland. The salt from the ocean was in the air but the scent from the trees was missing. Nothing felt natural.

"Be on guard." "You realize how silly you sound saying that. Of course I'm on guard."

She cut her eye toward him but didn't comment. The duo moved swiftly but cautiously, blasters already in hand. In the distance, she could hear Lewis and Lassiter talking.

"One boat is here." "How do you know? I can't hear anything but us and the birds." "Sonic hearing." "Of course. What was I thinking?"

They climbed up a steep hill and got the first visual of Rudo's cabin. No lights shined through the dirty windows. Shutters were broken and falling off the structure. Ember could make out cracks in the chimney.

"Sure doesn't look impressive," Liam commented. "Looks can be deceiving."

Lassiter and Lewis flanked their right. Morris and Nova were several yards behind them on the left. As Ember and Liam started their approach, the woods fell silent.

"Stop." She held her arm out and Liam's chest bumped into it.

"Ember, what the-"

"Shh!"

She leaned her head to the side and closed her eyes. After a moment, Liam sighed.

"I still don't hear-"

"Look out!" Ember yelled, shoving Liam aside.

She barely rolled to the right before a tree branch landed between where the couple once stood. The tree seemed to groan as the branch moved, attempting to crush her again. Yells off to the right let her know Lassiter and Lewis were in a similar predicament. She rolled out of the way and fired her blaster at the tree. The laser should've burned a hole through the middle but instead, the tree seemed to digitize and the shots went through without damage.

For a moment, she relaxed. "It's a hologram."

She bent down to help Liam up and a branch landed hard across her shoulder blades. She collapsed on the ground, groaning in pain.

"Wilson!" Morris yelled as he ran up to them.

She rolled onto her back just as a tree smacked Liam unconscious. Morris picked up the Air Force Major, draping him across his shoulders. Ember pulled herself up to her feet and they broke out into a run.

"What are these things?"

"No idea." Ember looked over her shoulder to see several trees chasing them.

Something struck the back of her head. The greenery had started throwing apples. Another tree jumped out at them, causing them to turn right. More foliage chased them as apples, pine cones, and rocks whizzed by their heads.

"Turn around!" Ember yelled.

"What? Why?"

"These things are trying to steer us in this direction. Change course."

Ember turned quickly and rushed at their pursuers, catching them off-guard. Morris followed behind and they turned to the right. They dodged projectiles and branches as the cabin once again came into view. She increased her speed as the attackers multiplied. Ember jumped through a side window to the cabin with Morris behind her.

At least, she thought he was. Neither Morris nor Liam was in the room when she stood up and shook the glass out of her black hair.

"Where am I?"

She wasn't sure what she was expecting, but it wasn't this. The walls were made of marble, not wood. The floors were also in the same cold gray marbled stone. The broken glass littered the ground but the walls were smooth. There wasn't any evidence of a window ever existing. Wooden crates lined the far wall and a dim light bulb hung low from the ceiling.

"This is really strange."

She tried to call to her team but no one answered the comm. Ember grabbed the brass door knob and paused, trying to listen for any noise. Nothing could've prepared her for what was on the other side of the door.

***

"Whoa!"

She was standing on a platform next to a staircase. Several other doors were along the pathway. Past an iron railing was a massive collection of moving parts. Gears slowly turned on the huge machine. Huge long and thick cable wires hung from various surfaces of gray metal. It almost looked like the inside of an engine. She looked down from the railing and the machine kept going, seemingly with no end. Looking up, she could see more floors identical to the one she was on.

"Anyone read?" She asked into the comm.

"Ember?"

"Liam! Where are you? Where's Morris?"

"No clue. I woke up to see us crash through a window after you but when I stood up, I was alone."

"Curious. What do you see?"

"I'm in a room with lime green walls and yellow spotted carpet. Did you see the large machine?"

"Looking right at it."

"I must be on the forty-third floor."

"What makes you say that?"

"Number on the door says forty-three."

Ember looked behind her and the door showed the number fifty-seven on it.

"Wilson, come in."

"I read you, Lewis. What's your status?"

"Look up."

Lewis waved down at her from two floors above.

"Stay right there," she ordered.

Ember ran up the stairs, taking two at a time. They bumped fists at the top of the landing. "Where's Lassiter?"

"We were chased by trees in the forest. He couldn't keep up with me. I heard him yell and when I looked behind me, all I saw was a pile of leaves."

The crackle on their comm made them both relax as another of their team members checked in.

"Lewis or Wilson, come on."

"I read you, Nova. Where are you?" Ember asked.

"Morris and I are looking at a large glowing ball."

Ember and Lewis looked at each other dumbfounded.

"Yeah, I know. We don't get it either," Morris said. "One minute I was running with Wilson through a window. Next thing I knew I was alone in a strange room. I fell through a door in the floor and Nova cushioned my fall."

"Are you looking at a machine?" Ember asked.

"No," Nova answered. "We're in what looks like a storage locker. The lock on the door is unlike any security pad Morris has ever seen." There were sounds of something sparking followed by a groan. "I told you not to mess with the scanner."

"Is he all right?"

"Is he ever all right?" Nova joked. "Just got shocked is all. Yeah, he's fine. His hair is standing up though. Looks like he's seen a ghost and his hair is the color of one now."

"Ross, are you hearing this?" Lewis asked.

"Big glowing ball and Morris' hair turned white. I'm almost to your location."

"Do you think it's weird we haven't run into anyone else yet?" Ember asked.

Lewis nodded. "I was just thinking the same thing."

Once Liam met up with them, they began to investigate the other rooms on the floor. Each of them seemed to be created from different materials. Some were empty. A few had crates similar to the ones in the room she came in.

"How are we going to get out? Our ship is gone and we can't signal to General Blanchard," Liam stated.

"We need to find the weather machine first," Lewis pointed out.

"This place has got to have some sort of communications array. We just need to find it." Ember opened up a crate as she spoke.

Inside was filled with topography and weather charts. She flipped through one as realization hit her.

"Michael, come take a look at this."

His bottom lip twitched when she called him by his first name but he shrugged it off. He flipped through several of the pages she handed him.

"Charts of the United Kingdom. So?"

"I think these are reports generated from this place."

He looked at her blankly for a moment before his purple eyes lit up.

"We're standing inside the weather system."

Ember nodded. "I think so."

"Great! Now we can destroy it and ..."

"Not so fast. The West Coast is still frozen, remember? We need to figure out how to use this thing and reverse it."

Liam sighed and rubbed his temples. The trio walked out onto the platform outside the room, discussing their next course of action when a menacing voice rang out, echoing throughout the walkway.

"Welcome, Amethyst team. So glad you could join me."

"Rudo." Ember hissed.

"Glad to see being in stasis hasn't changed you, Ember Wilson."

"He can hear us?" Liam questioned.

"Of course, Major Ross. Yes, I know who you are. Congratulations on being the last surviving member of the Air Force team. General Blanchard must be so proud."

"Quit playing games and show yourself!" Lewis yelled.

"Ah, Michael Lewis. You're just as brilliant as ever. Are you enjoying yourself?"

"Cut it out."

Laughter echoed around them. "You must know you have no hopes of leaving here alive. The least you can do is entertain me before I end you."

"Rudo, just wait until I get my hands on you." Ember paced on the platform, seething in rage.

"Looking forward to it, Ember. I have something special just for you."

"Are we going to fight, or do you plan to talk me to death?"

"All in due time. But first, let's change the playing field."

The ground beneath them began to rumble. The air turned cold and icicles began to form on the walls.

"Move!" Ember yelled as chunks of the ceiling began to fall.

She ran and jumped off the railing, grabbing onto a pair of thick wires and began climbing. She looked down to see the platform they were on was gone. Lewis followed Ember's lead and had jumped on a gear. As it rotated, he pulled himself up and jumped to the next level above them.

Liam wasn't as lucky. He landed hard on the walkway underneath the level, barely avoiding getting crushed by debris. "Ember!"

"Liam! Are you okay?"

"I think so."

"Stay there, I'm coming to you."

"Don't worry about me. I'm fine. Go find Rudo."

Rudo's laughter rang in her ears as the wires she was on vibrated.

"So touching. Well, if you're offering me your life, least I can do is accept."

Ember gripped the wires as the whole area began to shake violently. She pushed away from the cables and let go, free falling several yards and landing gracefully on the platform next to Liam. His face was caked in blood and dirt. His uniform was badly ripped and he looked out on his feet. The floor shook as two robots rolled toward them, stopping several feet from the couple, pulling out weapons, and opened fire. Liam groaned as he was hit in the shoulder. The shots didn't faze her as she rushed at them, destroying one with a swift kick and picking the other up, tossing it over the railing.

"The ability to withstand blaster fire comes in handy," Liam muttered.

"I have thick skin. Your shoulder looks bad." She frowned.

"I may not have super-freaky healing powers, but I'll be all right."

"You're coming with me."

"No, I'll only slow you down." Liam shook his head emphatically. "I'm going to be fine. Go, Ember. Finish this."

He grimaced briefly as he reached up and stroked her cheek, looking into her eyes.

"You're going to get yourself killed." Her voice shook as she swallowed the lump forming in her throat.

"Better me than you. Get out of here."

When she didn't move, he attempted to shove her.

"You silly ass, go!"

"Wilson, I got him." Nova's voice stated over the comm.

"Don't die on me." She pressed her forehead to his. "We're not finished yet."

"I love you, too." Liam grinned.

***

Ember scaled up the cables after Nova pulled Liam out of danger. She called out to Rudo but this time received no response. Lewis reported that he found a room filled with monitors and a hot coffee at a desk.

"He was here. Must've seen me coming and ran off."

"Use the monitors to locate him."

"I tried but haven't seen him. He must be someplace without a camera."

Ember growled. "Any insight?"

"This place is phenomenal." He paused. "Keep climbing."

"Do you have something?"

"There's a door with green light emitting underneath it. No camera is in the room. It's three levels above you."

She quickly scaled the wires, jumping to the railing and pulled herself up. The door Lewis was referring to was basking in a bright green light.

"Ember ... be careful."

"Aren't I always?"

"I'm being serious."

"All right ... thanks, Michael."

It didn't surprise her when she found the door unlocked. She knew Rudo would be expecting her. She felt almost giddy to finally be having a showdown with the rogue scientist.

The door swung open with ease. Her hand flew over her eyes as the green light blinded her. When she was able to focus, she saw the light was coming from a console which took up the entire back wall. Rudo stared at the monitor, not turning around as she crept in the room.

"Did you really think you would defeat me so easily?"

"Yeah, I kinda did."

Her blaster was trained on the back of Rudo's head as he held up his hands.

"This is not very sporting of you, is it?"

"You want to talk sporting?" She snarled. "I'm giving you the same chance you gave the residents of D.C."

"Ah, I see. In your mind, this is proper. Justice will be served."

As Ember's finger moved to pull the trigger, Rudo's arm flew back, connecting with a back hand. He spun around, bringing his elbow to her wrist. The blaster went off, bouncing against the walls before breaking the door. He grabbed her arm, forcing her to drop her gun. She punched him twice, blood spewing from the corner of his mouth. A swift kick to his ribs gave them some much needed distance. She charged at him, ramming her shoulder into his stomach, running him into the computer desk. Rudo groaned and coughed, clubbing her in the back and across the shoulders. Ember took a slight step back before jamming her shoulder into him again. He punched her into her throat which made her back off of him, coughing hard.

Rudo kicked Ember in the stomach before pulling out a knife dripping with a yellow substance, aiming for her chest. She grabbed his wrists, twisting them to the side. Another punch connected with his jaw and she lunged for her weapon. She twirled around quickly and fired.

Shock filled Rudo's eyes and he looked down to the perfect little hole she left on him. He stumbled back, color draining from his face as the light left his eyes.

"Ow." She pulled out the knife he managed to plunge into her side and tossed it down. The yellow substance tingled her skin for a moment before disappearing. Purple blood washed over her hand as she applied pressure to the wound, knowing it would close up within a matter of moments.

Ember bent down to ensure Rudo was dead before calling to her team over the comm. "It's over. Rudo's dead."

***

The team met up with her several minutes later. Everyone looked beaten up but none of the injuries looked severe except for Liam's shoulder.

"You're bleeding!" Liam exclaimed, gently touching her hand covering the wound.

"It's nothing." She shrugged it off. "I'm already healing."

"Are you sure?"

Ember lifted up her shirt, just enough to show off her flat stomach. "See? The hole is already closing."

His hand gently caressed her skin. "Amazing."

"It's nothing." She waved it off. "Kind of tingles actually."

She adjusted her shirt, turning attention to Morris. She waved her hands toward the console and stepped out of the way. "Morris, have at it."

Morris ran his hand through his short hair before rubbing his hands anxiously. Monitors lit up as he typed several commands.

"Do you know what you're doing?" Nova asked.

"Not in the slightest," he admitted. "But this is going to be fun."

He used the planet's orbiting satellites to coordinate with Rudo's machine. Washington, D.C. appeared on the screen.

"Wow, it's really frozen," Ember remarked in awe.

Everything was ice. Rudo struck without warning when he used the machine. It looked like someone had hit pause on a holographic entertainment program.

"It looks so strange. Even the people are fozen solid," Lewis said.

"Do you think they'll be okay once Morris undoes this?" Liam asked.

Ember frowned. "I hope so."

"Here goes nothing," Morris muttered, pressing a few buttons.

The sky turned from grey to red, then bright red. A bright flash lit up the screen. As it dissipated, so did the ice. The people fell over, cars which had been frozen while in drive, crashed into one another. Snow quickly melted, but the ground wasn't ready to absorb it. Water began to flood the area as people cried out. Steam seemed to fill the air from the ground and building. In a matter of moments, the water was gone.

"Uh, oh," Morris murmured.

"What did you do?" Ember asked.

His hands worked vigorously against the keyboard. The sky went from red to light blue. Morris sighed in relief, leaning back in his chair.

"It's going to be okay."

"What happened?" Lewis questioned.

"I kind of made it go from below zero to over one hundred degrees in the matter of seconds," Morris sheepishly said.

"Morris!" Ember exclaimed.

"Hey, this is a complicated system here."

"And now?"

"It's a brisk fifty-seven degrees."

"Well, at least we don't have to worry about giving people second degree burns."

Chaos erupted as car accidents ensued. Confusion was wide-spread. It would take hours to get everything straightened.

"Can you make contact with Lunis Two?" Ember asked.

"Uh ... yeah. Shouldn't be a problem, actually."

After several more keystrokes, the worried face of General Tom Blanchard appeared on the screen. Upon seeing Ember, he seemed to relax.

"General, I'm here to report our mission is a success," Ember said.

"When the sensors reported D.C. unfroze, I had hoped. Is everyone all right?"

"We are in need of medical attention, but no one is dire."

"Good to hear. Expect me in an hour."

Ember bowed her head in a sign of respect to the military commander when General Blanchard arrived. A team of scientists followed behind and worked to restore California without harm.

"Yeah, sure. Now that I figured it out, they swoop in," Morris murmured.

"Aw, buddy. It's okay." Nova patted his shoulder. "You saved Washington."

Morris grinned. "I did, didn't I?"

"Do you want to stay behind with the science nerds as they research, or do you want to come back to the space station with us?" Ember asked.

"No chance. Let's get the hell out of here."

* * *

"Earth owes you a great deal of gratitude," General Blanchard said in the conference room.

"Just doing our duty, sir." Ember stood at full attention, wearing a clean uniform.

"With the machine still intact, we'll be able to use it for what we originally thought it was designed for. Earth will finally have a climate conducive to growing our own food again on land. Soon, we will no longer have to rely on other planets to sustain us."

"That's good news, General. But what happens now? Are we to go back in the stasis tubes?"

"No, Ember. President Packer has dismissed all charges against Amethyst. You and your team are to be celebrated as heroes and Major Ross' fallen comrades are to be given special honors."

"Thank you, sir."

He placed his hands on her shoulders, smiling warmly at her. "How are you feeling?"

"Fully healed and ready for the next commission."

"That's my girl."

Ember returned his grin. "Yes, I am."

"Well, you've been granted a little time off if you want to take a vacation."

"I've got no place in particular to go."

"How about traveling with Major Ross?"

"Dad." Ember looked at him scornfully. "Don't think because we're getting on better terms you can stick your nose where it doesn't belong."

"Ember, I know it's difficult for you to let me in, but don't be afraid to open your heart to him. Liam loves you very much and I would be willing to bet the stars on my collar the feeling is mutual."

She glared at him for several moments, unhappy he was butting into her love life, but softened her expression. "Thanks, Dad." It was still weird to call him anything other than General but it felt good to have her father back.

"You certainly don't have to. It's just a suggestion from an old man. Take it from me, Ember. When you find something special ... don't let it go." His eyes glazed over as he spoke. "I lost mine a long time ago. There's not a day that goes by I don't miss your mother. Time is a special commodity which we don't have a lot of. Don't waste it."

"Thank you, I appreciate it."

***

She met up with Liam in their room, wrapping her arms around him tightly.

"You don't know how difficult it's going to be to leave you," he muttered as he kissed her neck.

"What do you mean?" She pulled away from him, studying his expression.

"My assignment here is over. I'm supposed to report to Washington in two days."

"General Blanchard ... my father granted us some leave. Would you like to go on a vacation with me?"

"Are you serious?" His eyes danced with excitement. Ember nodded. "Hell yeah! Let's go!"

He kissed her lips, running his hands down her arms and sides. Their shirts were discarded as they started toward the bed.

Suddenly the room started to spin. Ember pulled away, trying to focus. Her heart started to race and she was out of breath.

"Ember, what's wrong?"

Her hand went to her right side, the same spot where she had been stabbed by Rudo. The wound was re-opened after being fully healed. Thick, yellow fluid seemed to ooze out of her, coating her hand. Her entire body went limp, too weak to sit up. Liam called to her but she couldn't respond.

The last thing she saw before losing consciousness was Liam's terrified brown eyes.

***

Ember groaned as she started waking up. She felt sorer than she had in a long time. Every muscle in her body was stiff. Her body protested as she tried to stretch. Her eyes fluttered open, quickly adjusting to the bright light.

She was in a hospital bed. Sterile white walls, gray floor, and a TV perched in a corner. Liam sat in a chair next to the bed, looking bored at the TV.

"Hey," she said, surprised how weak her voice sounded.

He spun around in his chair, smiling. "Hey!"

"What the hell is going on?"

"Ember, I don't want you to freak out ..."

"Why would I -"

Out of the corner of her eye, she saw a blood bag connected to an IV in her arm. She gasped as she pointed to the bag.

"That blood is red!"

"Yes, Ember, listen to me -"

"Why is that blood red?"

"Honey, calm down -"

"Don't tell me to calm down! Liam, what the -"

Liam covered her mouth with his hand. "Okay, I understand you're freaked out, but you've got to listen to me. Now I'm going to take my hand away. Are you going to listen?" Ember nodded. "Good." He dropped his hand, stroking her cheek. "We're still figuring a lot of it out. What we do know is whatever was on the knife Rudo stabbed you in was ... well, for a lack of better word, poisonous."

"Poisonous?"

"Yeah. It attacked your blood cells. It was fast working and nearly killed you. The only way to save you was ..."

"Was what?"

"With a blood transfusion."

"I don't understand."

Liam sighed. His lips brushed against her temple before he sat back down in his chair.

"Whatever that yellow stuff was targeted the cells affected by the Genesis Project. Then it destroyed everything else. So the doctor did what he had to do to save you."

The wheels in her head turned as she considered his words. Her heart dropped into her stomach as realization washed over her. "My blood is no longer purple. Are my eyes?"

He swallowed. "No. They're blue."

Hot tears flowed down her cheeks. Rudo said he had something special planned for her. And that something made her ordinary again.

CHAPTER EIGHT

"Ember?"

Ember Wilson sat motionless in an oversized comfy chair as she gazed out the window of her apartment in West Virginia. A dark green blanket was draped around her shoulders, accentuating her naturally blonde roots on top of her otherwise raven head. Heavy bags bulged under her sullen eyes from lack of sleep. A light snow had dusted the mountains overnight and now the gleam from the sun reflected from the mountain tops and trees, creating a glow on the fresh powder. Passersby huddled tight in their jackets and quickly walked to get out of the brisk cold.

"Ember?" The voice from behind grew more insistent. She continued to ignore him.

It had been two months since she had been medically cleared from the hospital. Two months since an enemy had plunged a knife laced with a substance known as croceus into her side and had nearly ended her life. Two months since the poison had done the job Dr. Clayton Rudo intended and robbed her of the thing that had made her special.

It had been two months of hell.

She was once the leader of a genetically enhanced group known as Amethyst. She was once practically invincible. Now she was just average. The word *average* kept rattling around in her brain, causing her to involuntarily shudder.

The croceus ran through her blood, creating a toxic substance that attacked every fiber of her being. The only way the medical team could save her was to do a blood transfusion to clear her body. In the end, it took away everything the Genesis Project had given her.

She didn't look away from the window when she heard a shifting of feet and the scratch of a chair dragging across her carpet. A familiar touch grazed her skin and ran a finger from her wrist to her triceps. Goosebumps formed under his stroke. Still she ignored him.

"Come on, sweetheart. I really need you to talk to me."

She growled at the term of affection. The finger stroking stopped. A heavy, deep sigh blew in her ear as he pulled away. There was a chuckle from the other side of the room.

"You think you're going to reach Wilson like that? And here I thought you knew her."

"Shove it, Lewis."

"Oooh, testy! You just hate it when I'm right, don't you, Major?"

"There are many things I hate about you, Lewis."

A deep laugh echoed throughout the room. The air beside her moved as Major Liam Ross leaped out of his chair and advanced on Michael Lewis, Amethyst's second-in-command. There was a scuffle, the sound of objects falling off of her dresser and glass breaking rang out. A loud grunt followed.

"You need to get a handle on yourself, Ross," she heard Lewis hiss. "I don't know what you think you're going to accomplish by attacking me, but I could render you unconscious with a flick of my wrist right now. Don't think I won't."

Another sound she didn't recognize followed, but Ember didn't turn her head to see the commotion. Liam coughed several times and she heard a wheeze in his voice.

"You're a jackass," Liam grumbled.

"Yeah, well, I'm an honest one."

Ember sat close enough to the window to feel the chill from outside. Another shiver ran down her spine, reminding her how vulnerable she was. She clenched her hands until her knuckles turned white. Ember looked down at her palms and dug her nails in, breaking the skin and causing small droplets of blood to rise to the surface. Two months ago, she would've already started healing. Now the blood stayed on the surface until she wiped it on her khaki pants. She didn't care about the small streak of red blood.

Red blood. It used to be purple.

Her eyes had once been purple. They had been a gorgeous shade of deep purple – the same shade as her group's namesake. Now they were back to their original blue, the color dulled from her pain and grief.

"Don't do that," Liam said as he reclaimed his spot in the chair next to her. He reached for her hands but she pulled away from him. He sighed. "Why won't you look at me?"

"You really don't get it, do you?" Lewis asked. "She doesn't want you to see her."

Ember clicked her tongue on the roof of her mouth three times and nodded.

"If that's how she feels, then she should tell me herself."

"Go away," Ember said in a huff.

"What?"

She finally turned to face him. Liam's short brown hair was slicked back away from his face. He had large bags under his eyes, evidence he hadn't slept recently. An uncharacteristically scratchy beard had started to grow. His brown eyes were filled with worry as he searched her face. The tortured look etched on his face shot through her like a hot poker. Her bottom lip trembled as tears threatened to fall, but she only knew one way to free him from his pain. She swallowed hard and steeled her nerves, hoping the guilt she felt wasn't shining through her eyes.

"I said go away, Liam."

He recoiled as far back in the chair as he could. Ember shrugged before turning her attention to the window, hoping to seem dismissive as regret flooded her.

"I love you, Ember, but you can't keep pushing me away. One day, you're going to look around and see that I'm not there."

"Oh, let that day be today," Lewis said.

"I've had just as much of you as I can stand," Liam hotly replied.

"Enough," Exasperation seeping in Ember's voice. "You both need to cool it. Liam, you wouldn't last in a fight with him, and Lewis, quit trying to goad him."

"Oh, but it's so much fun!" Lewis snickered.

Ember rubbed her temples. "You both are giving me a headache."

"You want me to leave you alone? Fine." Liam stood up. "Call me if you need anything."

"Don't hold your breath," she replied.

She closed her eyes as she heard the door slide closed. She mentally heard the door slam, even though it wasn't capable of the action.

I don't know how to make him see. She closed her eyes as her thoughts bombarded her. *There's no way for him to know where I'm coming from. He can't be here. Not like this.*

Ember hadn't admitted to anyone how strong her feelings for Liam were, but he had only known her as the powerful leader of the Intergalactic Security Commission's elite field group. He had never seen her weak before. She didn't want him to see her like this.

"He'll be fine," Lewis said as he sat down in the chair next to her. "Eventually he'll get it."

She felt so lost. When she had signed up to be a part of the Genesis Project, she had resigned her commission with Earth's military. Now she wasn't cut out to be a part of the team. She didn't know what to do.

The Genesis Project had been the brain child of Dr. Madison Brooks, a renowned scientist who had lived over a thousand of years ago. When the ISC first began, it had been a secret organization. The creator, Charles Westlake, had thought the world wasn't ready to know Earth's position in the galaxy. For every person who became an ISC agent, a clone had been created to take over the life of the individual. History states when a heavily advanced race called the Synth had come to Earth to take over, the ISC went public. Since then, clones were no longer necessary. Dr. Brooks, who legend had it, had been a clone herself, had devised a formula to improve on natural abilities. However, the technology to implement it hadn't been available, so she never saw the Genesis Project to fruition.

Now there were five teams with special abilities. Amethyst was the top tier. Alexander Nova was the best pilot the ISC had. Bryan Morris was the tech guru. Michael Lewis was the strategist. And Ember was the leader and warrior.

And now she felt weaker than she did before she began basic training.

"Everything is going to be okay, Wilson," Lewis assured her. "You just have to have faith."

"What is that?"

"I don't know. Just seemed the thing to say."

"Do yourself a favor and shut up while you are ahead."

"What I don't understand is why you can't just undergo the process again."

"If I could, I would."

In truth, the process she underwent for Genesis had been extremely painful. Even if the ISC could duplicate the procedure quickly, she wouldn't live through it in her current condition. Emmitt Stewart, the commander of the ISC, had assured her steps were being taken to recreate the process, but it would take months, possibly up to a year, to get it ready.

Ember and Lewis sat in silence for several minutes. She stared out the window as snow started to fall.

"Will you hate me if I ask you a question?" Lewis inquired, breaking the quiet.

"Probably, but go for it."

"Is the thing between you and Major Tight-pants over?"

Ember sucked in a breath before nodding. "Yeah."

"Poor guy. He's going to have a hard time getting over you."

"Poor guy? Weren't you just mocking him?"

"Yeah, I was. Still, I've been in his shoes."

"You talk as if I'm something."

"Ember, you're everything."

She snorted in exasperation and rolled her eyes. Lewis sucked on his bottom lip before he stood up and nodded.

"Look, I know I'm pressing my luck here, but I've got to try. You've been through hell, Wilson. A weaker person wouldn't be on their feet. Regardless of what color your eyes are, I still feel the same about you. My heart remains the same." She swung her eyes up to meet his. "And it will never change."

He held her gaze for several quiet moments before he rubbed a hand over his face and nodded.

"Again, I knew it was a long shot. I just had to let you know how I feel."

"Everyone is always so quick to talk emotions," she said, bitterness resonating in her voice. "I'm not interested in hearts and flowers and shit. I'm not that kind of girl."

"Thanks for making me a bigger girl than you."

Ember grinned. "It's not difficult."

She stood up and approached him. She stared into his eyes for several moments, seeing her reflection in his. For the moment, she felt relieved he wasn't looking at her with sad, pitiful eyes. A hunger shined through, making her bite her lip reflexively. She grabbed him by the back of his neck and pulled his lips down to meet hers. Their kiss was hungry, primal. Her skin began to heat up as Lewis separated her lips with his tongue, deepening their embrace. She moaned as she grabbed a fistful of his shirt, their tongues wrestling for dominance. In one swift motion, she lifted his shirt and pulled it over his head. Her fingers traced the line of his well-toned abs before he grabbed her hand, bringing her fingers to his lips and biting down on the pad of her thumb. Ember whimpered and her head fell back. Lewis took the opportunity to kiss down her neck, nibbling on her tender flesh. Her nails grazed his skin as she gave in to him. He picked her up by the waist and she wrapped her legs around his hips.

She didn't want words. She didn't want hearts and flowers or have anyone looking pitifully at her. She needed to be reminded of what it was like to be powerful. They fell on the bed and Ember rolled to put Lewis on his back. She discarded her shirt and bra, slapping his hand away as he reached up to touch her. She clicked her tongue on the roof of her mouth and wagged her finger. She straddled his waist and wiggled his hips, satisfied as his body bucked underneath her. He reached up to touch her again, but she captured his wrists. She leaned forward, pinning his arms above his head.

"Ember, you're killing me," he groaned.

"You will touch when I say you can."

She let him go to reach into her night stand and pulled out a pair of magnetized handcuffs. She smiled as she heard the tell-tale click, letting her know they were locked. Lewis grimaced and tried to separate his hands, but the magnet in the cuffs wouldn't budge.

"Hands above your head," she instructed.

"Come on, Ember."

"Above your head," she repeated, enunciating her words.

Lewis sighed as he complied with her orders. She reveled in the wave of authority and dominance she had over his body as she removed the remainder of their clothing.

For the first time in two months, Ember felt like she was in control. She had Lewis at her mercy. He looked up at her with so much trust and wonder in his purple eyes. She relished in the feeling as their bodies finally merged.

Afterward, Ember stared up at the ceiling and counted the cracks in the plaster. The high she had prior to their sex was gone. Left in its wake was the overwhelming feeling of loneliness and guilt. The covers were pulled up over her chest. Lewis sat on the edge of the bed and began getting dressed.

"Are you okay?" Lewis asked.

"Right as snow."

She hoped to sound clear and confident, but she could hear her voice falter. A hand was placed above her knee, but she rolled away.

"So, it's like that?" Lewis's voice was dark. "That's all it was?"

"What did you expect?" she sharply questioned. "You know how this goes."

"Yeah, right. I'm probably the only person on this planet who can relate to you, and you're shutting me out, just like you shut Ross out."

"You really think so?" Ember sat up, crossing her arms over her chest as she glared. "Where do you get off? You think you can relate? On what planet could you possibly understand? You still have amethyst coursing through your veins!"

"Because I know what it's like to feel ordinary and then feel invincible. I still remember what it was like waking up in the morning before Genesis. Honestly, I don't know how you're still standing. I get why you're depressed. You have every reason to be. But Ember, I've seen you at your best, and I was there at your worst. This isn't it."

His words struck her hard. Ember rubbed her face with her hands and took a deep breath.

"We've always had a connection, Ember." He reached over and ran a finger down her arm. "Even before all this. You were the reason why I volunteered for the Genesis Project, remember?"

"Yeah, I remember."

"I knew you before, and I know you now. Ross can't be there for you like I can, so let me."

She looked hard at him for a moment before grumbling.

"Liam is right. You really are an ass."

"Why? Because I make sense?"

"Shut up."

Lewis laughed. "I'll take that as a yes." He leaned over and kissed the tip of your nose. "I'll see you tomorrow."

She slapped him, but there was no force behind the blow. "Don't get cocky."

He winked and got up from the bed. As soon as he left, Ember kicked back the remaining covers and gathered her clothes. After she dressed for bed, she brushed her teeth and washed her face. Ember patting her face dry as she gazed into the mirror.

What the hell am I doing? She wondered. *Where do I go from here?* She leaned in, nearly pressing her nose to the glass. *Who am I? My reflection doesn't match me anymore.* She sighed and opened up her medicine cabinet. After filling the cup of water on her sink, she grabbed a bottle of sleeping pills, popped two into her mouth, and downed the glass of water. She barely managed to crawl under the covers in her bed before drifting off.

***

Liam leaned against her door the moment it shut behind him. He slid down the metal to the floor, bringing his knees to his chest. Nothing could've prepared him for the wave of sorrow washing over him in that moment. He wasn't stupid by any means. When Ember got hurt, he expected her to push him away. Still, he hadn't expected to feel as empty as he did when he left.

He loved her. More than anything in the world, he loved her. Ember had a stubborn streak more prominent than her purple eyes. Liam closed his eyes tightly and corrected himself. Her once purple eyes.

She wasn't going to let him be there for her like he wanted. He knew it. If she was going to open up to anyone, the most likely candidate would be Michael Lewis. Ember wasn't the type to communicate with her words, but with action. He knew that, too. The idea that the woman he loved would possibly be with another man before the night was through was more than he could stomach.

Liam wanted nothing more than to pick himself up from the floor, march back into her quarters and. . . He wasn't sure how to finish the sentence. He couldn't force her to feel something she wasn't ready to admit.

He opened his eyes and let out a ragged breath he hadn't realized he'd been holding. He just had to keep faith that he was right. Ember would get through the pain she was in and she would come back to him. He hoped. Liam turned his head and pressed his ear to the door.

"Is the thing between you and Major Tight-pants over?" He heard Lewis ask.

There was a long pause, but he barely heard Ember reply, "Yeah."

So, that's it. There isn't anything left for me there. He slowly got to his feet and ran a hand through his uncombed hair, tugging at the tangles.

"I love you, Ember. You won't see me, but I'll always be here." He pressed his hand flat against her door.

He squared his shoulders back and gathered up all the pride he could muster, forcing himself to walk toward the teleportation room. He mentally patted himself on the back for not turning around.

Chapter Two

Ember woke up the next morning feeling rested for the first time in months. Lewis had already left, leaving a note behind. Her lips twitched, feeling both slightly annoyed and touched at the gesture. She crumpled up the paper before tossing it in the waste bin in the bathroom. After a sonic shower, she stood in front of her closet. She looked at the shirts hung neatly and organized. More than half of her wardrobe was the ISC uniform. Ember swallowed the knot of resentment threatening to choke her as she shoved a cluster of standard white shirts and grabbed the first civilian article of clothing she had, a dark green v-neck shirt.

At least I can still wear my boots, she thought as she buttoned up her jeans.

She ordered breakfast on the control console in her room before plopping down on the couch. To pass the time before her breakfast arrived, she turned on the holo. She sighed as she flipped through the different channels. An instructional program on space ship mechanics. A woman peddling jewelry. A children's program featuring a dancing yellow bear and a singing cat. A pop singer searching for the love of her life. *Nova was right. They didn't make entertainment holo shows like they did in the archives.*

"So bored!" She tilted her head up to the ceiling and growled.

Her doorbell chimed just as her stomach started to rumble. She jumped off the couch and pressed her thumb to the door panel.

"It's about time," she said in a huff as the door slid open.

Nova and Morris grinned as they pushed past her and entered, with Morris holding her breakfast tray in his hands.

"Well, make yourselves at home," Ember dryly greeted.

"Thanks, Wilson." Nova sat down in one of her oversized chairs and looked around. He took a piece of bubble gum from his pocket and popped it into his mouth. "Nice digs."

"Thanks. What are you doing here?"

"Delivering breakfast since you seem to refuse to eat in the mess," Morris replied.

"Get out, guys."

"You're not our boss anymore. Can't tell us what to do," Nova said before blowing a bubble with his gum.

"Go on, rub it in my face."

"Aw, Wilson, don't be like that." Morris rubbed the back of his neck.

"Yeah, we're here to cheer you up."

"Cheer me up? Nova, be serious."

"Can't. It's not in my DNA."

She crossed her arms over her chest, looking at the intruders crossly. Nova blew another bubble before sucking it back in. His red hair appeared freshly cut but the curls still made it look unruly. Morris had let his black hair grow longer. It now hung over his ears and he had to constantly brush strands away from his face. His wire-rimmed glasses fell to the tip of his nose and a smirk fell on his face as he pushed them back into proper position.

"You don't scare us so easily, Wilson. We're not like your major," Morris said.

"Don't do that." Ember frowned. "He's not my major."

"Are you kidding me?" Nova chuckled. "He's your little puppy. He would follow you to the ends of the Earth."

"Knock that off!"

"I'm serious, Wilson. He's been so torn lately. It's actually a little sickening."

"Great." A sinking feeling hit her stomach as she sat down on the bed. Morris nudged the plate of food closer to her, but she shook her head. "I lost my appetite."

"What, over him?" Nova leaned his head to the side, studying her. "I don't get it. Your bedroom reeks of sex, I can smell it from here, and yet you're ashamed?"

She pressed her lips into a thin line. *Damn them with their increased sensitivity to smells.*

"I wasn't with Liam last night," she admitted.

Both men looked slightly confused for a moment before realization hit. Nova clapped his hands together and laughed boisterously.

Morris clicked his tongue at her. "Shame, shame, Wilson. You know it's going to break his heart."

"It's over between me and Liam."

"Why? Because the playing field is leveled?"

"Something like that. Look, I don't expect you guys to understand."

"You're right. We don't understand." Morris narrowed his purple eyes at her. "We don't understand how you can go from the happiest we had ever seen you to being so miserable. We don't understand how you can shut out people who love you and are trying to be there for you. You're right. We just don't get it. Come on, Nova. Obviously Wilson wants to wallow."

"Please stay." She reached out to touch his arm but he pulled away from her.

"We weren't invited to your pity party, and frankly, this isn't you. We have other things we need to be doing." He took off his glasses and rubbed his eyes. "You are an incredibly selfish person."

"I'm selfish?"

"Like a little brat. Have you even thought about him?" Morris asked as he replaced his glasses and looked at her. "Ross lost his entire crew trying to help us take down Rudo. His. Entire. *Crew*. You've been through hell, but so has he. Where is your compassion?"

Ember's nostrils flared from anger as she balled up her fists.

"Where do you get off? Don't pretend to know what's going on. Until you can stand in my shoes, keep your trap shut."

"Fine." He squared his shoulders back. "Have it your way."

Morris walked briskly out of her room. Nova paused at the door before turning back to her.

"You know we're here for you. It's just hard to watch."

"Yeah, I guess."

"And Ross. . . Liam loves you, even if you aren't purple. And for the record, so do I."

"Thanks, Alexander."

He smiled when she used his first name. He walked over and gave her a brief hug before Morris yelled for him.

"I'm going to walk out now in a huff, okay?"

Ember nodded. Nova stroked her chin with his thumb and winked before standing up straight, sticking his chest out and stomping out of the room. She would've smiled if her heart wasn't hurting.

Morris's words struck her hard. She hated to admit he was right. She had been unfair to Liam and only made it worse by her betrayal last night with Lewis. She walked to her console and tried to search for Liam, but the computer showed he wasn't at the ISC.

"What's the meaning of this?" Commander Emmitt Steward demanded as she stormed into his office.

"Where is Major Liam Ross?"

"Major Ross?" He looked at her in confusion.

"I know it's easy for you to play dumb, but don't waste my time. Where is he?"

"Why would I know? He's Air Force, Agent Wilson. Major Ross is not in my jurisdiction."

"Some help you are," she grumbled as she swept out of his office.

Ember stormed back into her apartment and activated her communications server on her computer console. It beeped twice before the image of General Tom Blanchard appeared on the screen. He looked taken aback momentarily before he smiled.

"Ember! What do I owe the pleasure?"

"This isn't a personal call. Where's Liam?"

"I thought this wasn't a personal call."

"General, answer my question."

"Ah, so it's General. Well now, *Agent* Wilson, I am not obligated to inform the ISC of the whereabouts of my men."

"All right, Dad." Ember narrowed her eyes.

"Drop the attitude, Ember."

"Have we met?"

"You came to me for help, remember?"

"I know." She took a deep breath and sighed. "Okay."

A small smile tugged at the corner of his mouth. "From the beginning?"

"Fine." She clenched her teeth. "Dad, do you know where Liam is?"

"Of course I do. He returned to Washington this morning."

"Why?"

"He said he wasn't needed at the ISC, so he was reporting back to work."

Wasn't needed. She closed her eyes at his words. Guilt washed over her. Morris was right. She had done her job too well and Liam had gone back to Washington thinking she didn't need him. That was far from the truth. A struggle raged inside her heart, tearing at every inch of her soul. She didn't want him to see her weak, but she always needed him.

"Ember, what happened?"

Sadness filled her as she opened her eyes again and she prepared herself to admit her terrible behavior. "I sent him away."

"And you're surprised he listened?"

"I've been telling him to go away for a month and he hadn't yet!"

"There's only so much a man can take, Ember."

"I have been unfair to him."

"That's putting it mildly."

"Dad!"

"Tell me I'm wrong."

She glared before softening her expression. "I wish I could."

"Ember, everyone knows you're a warrior. You don't need to constantly show it. You are a strong, proud woman who hates admitting when she's wrong. And in this case, sweetheart, you are. Lower your guard every now and then. Not everyone is out to hurt you."

She grumbled as she looked down at the floor. He sighed before calling her attention back to the monitor.

"You need to focus on yourself to get better."

"I think focusing on me is what got me here."

"You're a hard person to get close to, Ember, and judging by these reports, you've been making things difficult. And not just for you, either."

"I know."

"I sympathize." His eyes softened. "I can't even begin to imagine what you've been through."

She managed to bite back a bitter comment. Her eyes still flashed though.

"Just because I haven't literally been there doesn't mean I don't feel empathy." He leaned back in his chair. "I have an idea. Why don't you get out of the ISC for a while? Come to Washington with me."

"And do what?"

That stopped him. He didn't have an answer.

"Sit around there like I would here, the only difference being Liam refusing to talk to me in person? No thanks."

"So talk to your commander. See if there is any busy work for you to do."

"I'm a solider," she said through her teeth. "I don't do busy work."

"You'd be amazed what you could do if you put your mind to it, Ember."

***

After speaking with her father, she decided he was right. Anything was better than sitting around her room. This time she didn't barge into Commander Stewart's office. He didn't hide his surprise when she came in after knocking.

"Agent Wilson, what can I do for you?"

"I was wondering if you had a task I would be able to do."

Shock spread across his face at her statement.

"You are volunteering?"

"I'm going out of my mind, Emmitt. I need something to do."

"As it so happens, yes." He stood up and pulled a data tablet out of his desk. She stood idle as he input commands and handed it to her.

She raised an eyebrow after she read it over. It was a class synopsis on Dr. Madison Brooks, a scientist who was still contributing to the ISC, over a thousand years after her death. "You're kidding."

"I think you would be good at it."

"You want me to teach?"

"Dr. Brooks is the reason we are all still here, Wilson. She was brilliant, resourceful, and resilient. I think you could learn a lot from her. Every ISC recruit has to take extensive classes on the history of the ISC -"

"Yes, Commander, I am aware. I took the classes once upon a time."

"So then you're well versed."

Truth be told, Dr. Brooks had always fascinated her. She had been a clone of Dr. Mackenzie Rhodes, another famous scientist in history. Both women had contributed to the success of the agency. Never before or since did a clone have that much impact.

"I know who she is."

"You know *of* her," he corrected. "I think this will be good for you."

"Is this an order, sir?"

Emmitt squared his shoulders as if anticipating a fight. "It's a recommendation."

She stared hard at him for a few moments. He sighed.

"I can understand your hesitation, but just think of this as a whole new challenge."

She raised her eyebrow. "A challenge?"

"Teaching is a skill, one you haven't mastered, even as a leader." She opened her mouth to speak, but he shook his head. "I know you've never had to be in a teaching role. Your men were already more than qualified before undergoing the Genesis transformation. Now you would be entrusted with the training of new recruits. It'll be a whole new experience for you."

She wouldn't admit it aloud, but the idea was intriguing. There were merits behind his proposal. He grinned when she didn't respond.

"Am I to take your silence as acceptance?" She nodded. "Very good. I would suggest beginning in the archives and pull up old mission files."

"Aren't the lesson plans already created?"

"Yes, but the plans are bare bones. Highlight the woman and you'll meet the very heart of the ISC."

"You are waxing rather poetically."

"That heartbeat is still beating today, Wilson."

She sighed deeply. "Yes, sir."

This was sounding more and more like grunt work than an assignment, but anything was better than sitting in her room staring out the window.

Chapter Nine

Ember left the commander's office and headed into the library. She avoided the stares as she walked past the rows of computer terminals. It was as if the people in the room knew she didn't really belong there. She hadn't been in the library since she graduated from the academy. She felt awkward as she pressed her thumb against the security plank outside the archives section. The plank turned green and she rushed inside.

Anyone could go to the library, but only a special few had the security clearance to get inside the archives. It was where the ISC's past was kept. Personnel files from agents, hundreds, if not thousands of years ago, old mission files, and videos, if they existed, were all housed in the archives. The room was dark, except for a soft glow from the console in the center of the room. She walked onto a platform and the console began to light up.

"Welcome, Ember Wilson," the computer greeted. "How may I help you?"

"Computer, I need data for Dr. Madison Brooks."

"Acknowledged." Instantly, a holographic image of the famous doctor stood before Ember. "Dr. Madison Brooks, born August 8th, 1982, died November 7th, 2068. Husband, Jonathan Brooks, born April 20th, 1982, died November 7th, 2068. Children —"

"Wait, Computer." The voice paused. "Dr. Brooks and her husband died on the same day?"

"They died several hours apart."

"Were they ill or injured?"

"Cause of death was listed as natural."

"For both of them?"

"Affirmative."

"That's odd."

Ember pressed her lips together as her mind rolled the information over and over. *I have heard of some animals that would die shortly after their mate. Is that what happened to them? Did they love each other that much?* The idea made Ember laugh. Such love didn't exist. The chime from the computer made her stop and focus.

"Computer, continue."

"Children, Lucas and —"

Ember sighed. "Bypass. Transmit comprehensive reports on missions to my tablet in my room."

"There are over six thousand mission files featuring Dr. Madison Brooks. Do you want all of the files transferred?"

Six thousand? "Are all the mission files connected with her lab reports?"

"Negative. There are four hundred lab reports."

Much better. "Narrow down the lab reports and her personal records from when Dr. Brooks first joined the ISC spanning over three years." She paused for a moment. "I also want mission files."

There was a brief hum before a small beep.

"Transfer complete."

Ember quickly retreated to her apartment. She flopped down on her couch and reached for her tablet lying on the end table. After it finished powering on, she received a message regarding new files. Everything was sorted into separate folders for easier access. She clicked on a folder marked 'Personal' and grinned at the lengthy list of audio files. Even though the audio was over a thousand years old, the ISC took great care in making sure everything was intact. Ember tapped on a link dated October 23rd, 2013 and leaned back on the pillow as an unfamiliar female voice began speaking.

"How is it possible I've only been here a week? I wanted to spend more time with Mack, but Jackson said she's keeping her distance. I wish I knew why. I have so many questions for her. Maybe that's why she's staying away. Maybe she doesn't want to have anything to do with me. I can't really blame her. This situation is . . . bizarre. Was it really only a week ago I was working in a call center? Now here I am, hiding from an alien race determined to kill me because I'm an easier target than my counterpart. And to top it all off, I'm being guarded by . . . well, I don't know what he is. He's," She paused. Ember heard a sharp intake of air. *"I need to keep John at arm's length. No good can come from exploring feelings, no matter how badly . . . the thought is insane! Jackson said clones don't form new attachments, but Mack never met John to my knowledge. At least not before the ISC and my . . . creation. So why do I get butterflies in my stomach when he looks at me? It can't be real."* There was another pause. *"I really want it to be real."*

The recording stopped, but Dr. Brooks's words hung in the air. Her heartfelt expression made Ember smile. She clicked on the next audio file and listened as Dr. Brooks recapped an attack on the ISC. She was detailed in describing the planet Dr. Rhodes, Agent Gray, and she escaped to. Ember was enthralled as the other woman spoke vividly. She hadn't been to the planet Aurora, but Ember could close her eyes and see the brown grass and purple sky. She was engrossed in file after file of stories. Dr. Brooks became more than renowned scientist. She was Maddie.

Ember felt like she *knew* the woman, as if they were in the room having a conversation. The more Maddie talked, the more Ember admired her. Not just as what she was, but *who* she was.

Her door chimed but she ignored it. Maddie was explaining how John proposed to her. The door started chiming insistently and Ember growled. She paused the recording and hit the control button on her end table to open her door. Lewis stepped in, looking quizzically at her.

"Is everything all right? I've been buzzing for around ten minutes. I was getting ready to do an emergency override on your door."

"Sorry. I've been listening to Ma —" she paused, clearing her throat. "I mean, Dr. Madison Brooks's personal files."

"Dr. Brooks?" Lewis cocked his head to the side. "Why?"

"Emmitt is having me teach one of the intro classes. He thinks it'll do me some good."

"You?" Lewis chuckled as he stood at the end of the couch. "A teacher?"

Ember glared. "Don't look at me like the thought is so completely farfetched. I can do this."

"Wilson, there isn't anything you can't do. No doubt in my mind."

"Except be in Amethyst."

He sighed before walking over to the other side of her on the couch and sat down. She moved over to give him room.

"Maybe Emmitt's right. Maybe this is exactly what you need to get your mind off of Amethyst."

"I don't want my mind off of it."

"I know you don't." He paused. "Even if you don't get everything back, you're going to be okay."

"Of course I am," she scoffed. "Yes, I know I've been difficult lately, but what else is new? I'm no walk in the park."

"So you're just biding your time."

"Until Emmitt can recreate the Genesis Project? You bet I am."

"Ember, there is a reason Amethyst has only four members. Hell, there is a reason why there are only five teams instead of twenty."

She swallowed hard. The rigorous process was still fresh in her mind, even years after undergoing it. There were over one hundred and fifty candidates. Thirty people endured the procedure for the Amethyst formula. The ISC was going to group the candidates into teams and have a squad on the ISC planets spread throughout the galaxy. Except only four survived. The ISC smartly discontinued the program.

Ember didn't need reminding. The thought had been rumbling around in her head for a while.

"My mind is made up," she said.

Lewis grumbled under his breath. He rubbed his forehead before nodding and hopped off the couch.

"I know what you need. Meet me in the training room in thirty minutes."

She looked skeptically at him. "You're serious?"

He grinned. "Thirty minutes, Wilson."

***

Ember was already in the training room when Lewis strode in. She sat cross-legged on the floor, bobbing her head to the heavy metal music blaring in the room. She uncurled her legs and rolled backward, using the muscles in her back and shoulders to roll to standing position, her arms swinging by her side.

"You look excited," Lewis commented.

"It's been a while since I've been in here."

"I know." Lewis strolled over to a wall lined with blasters of various sizes, grenades, knives, staffs, and swords. He walked the length of the wall, his fingers touching each weapon, until he came to a stop in front of a row of staffs. He pulled the and last one in the row off. "I think it's time you remembered who you are."

Ember raised an eyebrow and ran the tip of her tongue across her top lip. Lewis tossed one of the staffs at her. She caught it with both hands and pivoted on her feet to twirl. The staff was made of red oak, approximately five feet in length and was light-weight. The top of the weapon rested against her chest as she caressed it. Her hands fit easily into the grooves of the wood. She rotated it twice, getting the feel for it. Lewis stood in front of her with his staff cradled on the back of his neck and shoulders.

She recognized the staff from the training they underwent after the Genesis Project. A Keifler Stick, named after its creator, emitted an energy pulse when it connected with human tissue. A normal person would be rendered unconscious by the outburst of energy. For Amethyst, it felt like a tickle. It would take many shots to knock one of them out. She tapped the end of her stick twice and it glowed a dim purple before it grew brighter and crackled.

"Ah, so you remember."

She held up the lit end close to her face, feeling the energy flow from it as the hair on the back of her neck stood on end. They locked eyes as they set the sticks down and undressed down to their underwear. They always wore as little clothing as possible when they trained with the Keifler weapons.

"All right, rules," Lewis began. "Game is over after three hits."

"Only three?"

"This is a trial, Wilson. I'm not trying to knock you out."

She glared. "Fine."

"I'm letting you off easy in your fragile state. And because I'm such a nice guy, I won't activate my staff."

Ember pressed her lips into a thin line. "Fragile state?"

"You know." He grinned. "Your weakened physique."

She slashed the end of her lighted staff against his midsection. He blocked the blow, turning to bring his weapon down on her right shoulder. She moved out of the way, bringing the tip of her stick to his lower back. Lewis groaned as the purple light sparked against his skin.

"Not bad for a *weakened* woman."

"No." Lewis gritted his teeth. "Not bad at all."

They separated, giving each other distance. Ember dropped into a defensive stance with her left arm bent level to her chest, her feet shoulder width apart, and her right arm straight out holding the staff. They circled each other, their eyes locked. She twirled the staff before swiping at his chest. Lewis knocked her weapon away, striking her on the left shoulder before she could move.

"Gah!" Sharp pain reverberated through her arm. She winced and tried to rotate it. Her heart raced against her chest.

Lewis smiled. "Got to be more careful."

"That's one," she said.

"Yep, we're even."

She gripped the staff with both hands, moving to strike his wrists. At the last second, she flipped it up and struck him on the side of his head. Lewis stumbled back, cursing and sputtering. She didn't give him any time to recover before moving in. But he was ready for her tactics. The end of his weapon hit her mouth, busting her lip open, before swinging down and hitting the back of her knees. Ember fell on the mat, the air rushing out of her body as her staff fell out of her hands and rolled away. Lewis stood over her with his staff pointed at her face.

"And that's three," he said.

She looked up at him, breathing heavily. Her head pounded and sweat rolled down her face. She touched her lip and frowned at the red droplets of blood on her fingertips.

"So it is."

"Are you okay?"

She nodded. He tossed the staff aside and extended his hand, moving so she could get up. He gently touched her chin and frowned.

"I didn't mean to bust you open."

"It's a tiny cut."

"Looks pretty deep to me."

"Only because you're used to me healing already."

"It's going to take a while to get used to you not being -" He stopped, sucking in a sharp breath as she raised an eyebrow and crossed her arms over her chest.

"Me not being what? Finish your sentence."

He rubbed the back of his neck. "I can't."

"Finish your sentence," she ordered.

"Not being purple," he said, letting out a haggard breath.

She smacked his hand away and walked toward her clothes.

"Come on, Wilson. You know I'm sorry."

She snorted as she pulled on her pants. "Of course you are. Everyone is. The doctor is sorry he didn't catch the croceus poison before it nearly cost me my life. The nurse is sorry she aided in the blood transfusion. My father is sorry I can't rejoin my military commission. Commander Stewart is sorry he can't recreate the procedure. Liam is sorry he can't understand what I'm going through." She spun around, fire raging in her eyes. "And I'm sorry I let myself wallow in misery. But I'm not sorry anymore. Now I'm just angry!"

She stormed out of the training room, leaving her shirt on the floor and Lewis alone with his jaw hanging open. She brushed past the people in the hallway, not caring about the gawking looks she got for walking away in her bra.

Chapter Ten

A dozen tulips arrived at her door the next day. She left the box outside, not bothering to read the card attached. It was roses the following day. That time she shredded them and left the petals scattered outside. Lewis seemed to have taken the hint and no more followed. Word must've gotten around the ISC because no one approached her for more than a week. It suited her just fine. She was busy preparing for her introduction class at Commander Stewart's urging. With Morris still mad at her, her furious at Lewis, and Nova caught in the middle, she was alone. She preferred it that way. Things were less complicated. Still, she wasn't going to be deterred in her training. Instead of a human sparring partner, Ember had programed an android. The robot was designed to stop before inflicting real bodily harm to her and didn't talk. To Ember, it was the perfect partner.

Ember rubbed the bruise on her left shoulder from Lewis's strike a week and a half prior. Thankfully, it had dulled to a pale yellow and was only a minor ache. To her, it was a reminder of who she was now. She vowed it would be her last bruise. She had been improving with every session, regaining some of her lost agility, dexterity, and strength.

She looked hard at the reflection in her mirror. Her blue eyes still looked foreign to her and most of her natural blonde hair showed through the black dye. She sighed and sucked on her bottom lip. She pulled on her boots, tucked her hair into a baseball cap, and marched down the hallways into a part of the ISC she didn't normally venture into. She paused before stepping through a pair of glass doors into a crowded courtyard.

"The shopping district," she muttered under her breath.

The ISC had been designed so that agents would never have to leave the base unless they absolutely wanted to. The shopping district housed hundreds of different stores and boutiques. She waded through the crowd of Christmas shoppers until she came to a stop outside of a hair salon.

A male and female stylist chatted with each other while cutting their customers' hair. Two women were in the corner washing clients' tresses. Everyone stopped when Ember came in. The female stylist was tall and skinny with bronze skin, dark hair, and dark eyes. The male stylist was short and heavier set, with short blond hair and a goatee. The stylists looked her up and down, raising an eyebrow over her rumpled state of dress. She smiled politely and took a seat. The chatter continued as Ember absentmindedly tapped her foot on the tile floor. After the female finished with her client, she stood in front of Ember with her hands on her hips. She flashed a row of pearly white teeth and spoke with a Brazilian accent.

"How can I help you?"

Ember took off the baseball cap and shook out her mane of hair. The woman pressed her lips together in disapproval before waving her over to a sink.

"Let's get you fixed up."

"Thanks."

She was pushed down into a hard plastic chair and leaned back. Her neck rested in a depression on the back of the chair. A small cloth was placed over her face before water came on. The worker lathered up her hands and began washing Ember's hair.

"So, are you new to the ISC?"

"Not at all."

"Strange. I've never seen you around and I know everyone."

"Not everyone."

The woman chuckled. "Apparently so. What's your name?"

"Ember Wilson."

The woman stopped moving. The water splashed in Ember's face.

"Hey!"

"I . . . I'm so sorry! Forgive me."

"Everything okay?"

"Yes. Yes, of course."

"What's going on?"

"Nothing," she said before continuing to wash. "You have pretty hair. Nice and thick." Ember could tell she was changing the subject. "Why did you react like that when I told you my name?"

The water shut off. Ember felt the stylist squeeze her hair before a towel came around her shoulders. She sat up and eyed the stylist hard. The woman swallowed hard, appearing nervous.

"I'm sorry, I should explain."

"I would think so."

"My name is Beeka Thompas. I'm . . . special friends with Alexander Nova."

Ember's eyes lit up at the mention of his name. "You're the one sleeping with Nova?"

Beeka's cheeks turned pink as she nodded. "We've been together for a while now. Forgive my reaction, but

Alexander speaks very highly of you. But I must admit, the stories he tells," she blanched, "don't always paint you in the best light."

Ember pressed her lips together, feeling her irritation rise. Beeka's cheeks became a deeper shade of red.

"He does respect you," she clarified. "Like I said, he holds you in high esteem."

"Then what was this about stories?"

"You are a strong warrior. Unlike any other woman I have ever known to exist. You are dangerous, are you not?"

A chuckle bubbled in Ember's chest. *No wonder this woman was looking at me like I was going to take her head off at any moment.*

"Perhaps I was, but I'm not anymore. You can relax, Beeka."

"But you are his leader, no?"

Sadness filled her eyes and she shook her head. "I used to be."

Beeka eyed her warily. "Your eyes are not purple."

"No. They're not."

The fear Ember saw in Beeka's eyes changed to sympathy. She patted Ember's shoulder and helped her to her feet, leading her over to a salon chair.

"Are we dying your hair today?"

"No." Ember shook her head. "I want the dye out."

Beeka blinked several times. "I don't understand."

"I want the black out. Return to my natural color." Ember paused for a moment. "And a trim. Cut my hair to my shoulders."

Beeka's lips curled into a smile. "Beautiful."

A black nylon cape came around her front and snapped in the back. Ember relaxed in the chair as Beeka set to work. The Brazilian spoke warmly about Nova and of her cat named Kina. Ember yawned as she watched the stylist mix the hair coloring. *You would think with all the technology we have now, we would've figured out a way to not spend hours at a salon.* The liquid in the metal cup turned into a creamy white the more she stirred. Beeka grinned as she put on the latex gloves. The smell of chemicals filled the former field agent's nose and stung her eyes. Ember watched as the stylist would grab a collection of her long hair and used a brush to paint it with the white goop. The Brazilian hummed under her breath as she rolled the hair in foil.

"Put any more foil on me and I'll start picking up transmissions from the space station orbiting the Moon," Ember complained.

"Hush," Beeka admonished.

Ember grumbled in her chair but didn't comment further. She stared at the holo screen, sighing with boredom over a court show, as the dye did its job. Several customers came in and received cuts and perms. A young woman who also had her hair up in foil sat next to Ember and tried to engage her in conversation, but she had no interest in whatever the woman was babbling about.

"Ready?" Beeka asked as she approached. "Yes!" Ember exclaimed, quickly getting to her feet.

Foil was removed and thrown in a trash can. Another dry cloth was placed over her face as she got a second wash. Beeka wrapped a towel around Ember's shoulders and led her back to her chair.

"How do you want it styled?"

"Just blow dry it."

"You sure? It would look nice straightened."

"I think this is enough for today."

"We could curl it."

"My hair is naturally wavy. The cut and blow dry is fine."

"As you wish."

Beeka brushed the hair out and grabbed a small pair of scissors. Snip after snip, pieces of hair hit the floor at their feet. It had been three years since Ember had a haircut. The clippings piled up as the weight of the world seemed to lift off of her shoulders with each cut. Heat from the blow dryer hit her skin as the stylist finished up.

"Here you are! Good as new!" Beeka boasted as she spun Ember's chair around.

She couldn't believe her eyes. Ember blinked several times and the woman in the mirror did the same. She touched some of the wavy blonde strands which had been cut to her shoulder. The blonde was lighter than her natural color, but it would fade out. She ran her fingers through the silky tresses, trying to get used to it.

"You are very pretty," the stylist said.

Ember swallowed hard, not able to take her eyes off of her reflection. It was a face from the past. She didn't see herself in the mirror. She saw her mother, who she lost at a young age. She had very little memories of her, but a part of her lived on through Ember's eyes. Her father had said she was a spitting image of her and when she had signed up for the Genesis Project, he had accused her of losing his last connection to the love he lost when she'd changed. It was why she had dyed her hair black, to separate herself from him as much as possible. But it also separated her from her mother, a connection she had lost until now. Ember twisted some strands around her finger. *I can't believe it. Dad was right. I really do look like her. This is who I am now, and I can live with that.* Tears swelled up in her eyes, but she quickly blinked them away.

"You're not happy." Beeka frowned.

"No, it's not that. You did amazing."

The woman beamed. "Thank you."

***

A box was leaning against her front door when she returned from the salon. Ember contemplated leaving it outside, but curiosity got the better of her. She ripped open the box and tossed the brown paper on the floor. Her lips curled into a smile as she looked at the array of throwing knives inside. She set the box on her table and picked up one of the knives. It was lightweight with a swirl detailed engraving on the blade, and the handle fit easily in her hand. A note was placed inside the box which read, "I'm sorry. Please don't use me as target practice."

Her smile grew as she picked up the five throwing knives. *Forgiveness is good, but a lesson needs to be taught. Don't discount me, and don't you dare give me new weapons when I'm mad.* She tucked three of them into her boot, hid another in the sleeve of her shirt, and held the last one. "Computer, location for Michael Lewis."

"Michael Lewis is in the Training Room D," the computerized voice informed her.

"Perfect."

She quickly walked to the training center, coming to a stop outside of Room D. She squared her shoulders back before pushing through the swinging doors. She immediately spotted a shirtless Lewis standing in between Nova and Morris and threw a knife at his head. Lewis quickly brought his right arm up to defend himself, and the knife became lodged in his forearm. Nova and Morris's eyes widened as they backed away from Lewis to stand along the wall.

"What the hell, Wilson?" he growled as he pulled out the weapon. Purple blood began to drip from the gaping wound.

"I don't *need* target practice," she hissed.

"I can see that."

"You're an asshole, you know that?"

"I thought it was one of my better qualities."

"You *would* think that."

A twinge of jealousy struck her as the hole in his arm closed. She glared at him, pulling the second blade from the sleeve of her shirt. She ran her nail along the sharp metal, not taking her eyes off of him.

"You want to go, Wilson? We'll go," Lewis challenged.

She threw the knife at his shoulder and charged toward him. Lewis pulled it out of his skin and tossed it on the floor just as her shoulder collided with his midsection, and they hit the mats hard. Lewis rolled Ember onto her back but she quickly bucked him off. She rolled into a crouched position, smirking as purple blood dripped down his left side. Lewis threw the weapon back at her. She fell onto the mat and rolled to a standing position, completely avoiding the weapon.

"Wilson!" Morris yelled.

Ember pulled two knives from her boot and threw them at Morris and Nova. The blades found their marks in their shoulders, pinning them to the wall. She heard an irritated growl but didn't look over in their direction.

Lewis rushed at her, throwing a punch aimed for her nose. She managed to move out of the way, swinging her elbow to connect with his ribs. She clasped her hands together and clubbed him across the shoulder blades. Lewis took to a knee and groaned. She hooked his arm and rolled, flipping him onto his back. She straddled his waist, using her legs to pin him down. Lewis looked aggravated for a moment before his lips curled into a smile.

"Welcome back, Wilson."

***

Once the men had gotten cleaned up and dressed, the four of them went to one of the bars in the ISC.

"So, Wilson, what's with the blonde?" Nova asked as they slipped into a booth in the back corner. She shrugged. "Time for a change, I guess."

"Or you didn't want to appear all dark and scary when you start teaching," Morris teased.

"That too." She grinned at him. "You're picking on me again. Does that mean we're good?"

"Let's see," he began, counting on his fingers, "you burst through the doors and interrupted training because you're mad. You threw weapons at the three of us and sparred with Lewis. You actually knocked him on his ass, and you probably still have a knife tucked into your boot as we speak. I would say the old Wilson is back. Yeah, we're good."

"She didn't knock me on my ass," Lewis fumed.

"Right. On your back!" Nova cheerfully exclaimed.

"Ha ha." Lewis had a sour look on his face as he ordered drinks. "I could've rolled her off of me."

"Uh huh." Nova grabbed some peanuts from the bowl at the center of the table and popped a few into his mouth. "Just admit it. She got you, man. And she didn't need to be purple to do it." He flashed a bright, toothy grin. "She just needed to be Ember."

She could feel the blood rush to her cheeks. "Thanks."

Nova leaned forward and stared at her. "It's been a long time since I've seen you like this. It's a little weird, but also nice."

"Speaking of which, I met Beeka today. She seems real sweet. I'm happy for you."

She felt another stab of jealousy at the way Nova's eyes lit up at the mention of Beeka's name. She quickly pushed the image of Liam from her mind.

"Yeah, she's pretty great." He beamed. "She fusses at me about my hair, but other than that, she's the best."

"How do you cut your hair? It's not with scissors," Morris asked.

"You're just jealous of these gorgeous locks." Nova brushed a hand through his messy red hair.

"It looks like you took a sonic gardening tool to it."

Ember laughed at the teasing. It was great being among the guys again. For the most part, everything seemed back to normal. The camaraderie between them had returned. Being with them felt as natural as breathing. She was home again. But something felt . . . off. It tugged at the back of her mind. Ember couldn't shake the feeling that something was missing. She glanced around the table, mulling over the thoughts in her head. *What could it be?* And then it dawned on her.

It was Liam.

Chapter Eleven

"When we look at Dr. Brooks's achievements, it's amazing to think she was an ISC creation," Ember continued as she lectured the ISC recruits. "We've only looked in-depth at a fraction of the things she accomplished during her first two years."

Ember had been teaching the class for two weeks. To her surprise, she found she enjoyed it. Her students had been attentive and asked questions. Of course, it helped to have fascinating material to discuss. Teaching certainly renewed her respect and admiration for Maddie, and she hoped to pass it on to the ISC's newest recruits. It was a great way to honor the memory of the woman she had grown to idolize.

The last two weeks had been wonderful. When she wasn't teaching, Ember was training with Amethyst. It felt like old times. She was back in her groove again. At night, she took Lewis to bed. Usually after he left, she pulled up more of Dr. Brooks's diary files from the database. She fell asleep each night listening to the sweet sound of Maddie's voice talk about what was going on in her life as well as her personal thoughts behind mission files.

"If you are interested in more history, there is another course you can take. Our aspiring scientists may want to take advantage of it as it goes into details regarding the advancements made during the golden age of the ISC. Today is our last class, but I will leave you with one final assignment. I need everyone to write up your thoughts on the battle with the Synth and how it impacted the ISC. I know this is a big task, so you will have twenty-four hours to have it in my database. Those who do well will proceed on to basic training. Those who don't will have to retake this course. Good luck."

A low murmur swept through the crowd as she dismissed them. She sat on her desk and watched them leave. Through the crowd of people, she spotted a smug-looking Michael Lewis standing on the back wall.

"Good job, Wilson. You made it without maiming anyone. Honestly, I didn't think you had it in you."

"The only one in this room in danger of getting maimed is you, if you're not careful."

"Now that's not nice." He placed his hand over his heart, feigning hurt. "Your words wound as much as your actions."

She laughed. "What's up?"

His eyes twinkled as he approached her. He placed his hands on her desk, inches from touching her.

"I've got a surprise for you."

"And what's that?"

"The colony over on Sullalore need help. Seems the Kashe clan is starting trouble again."

Her eyes lit up. *A mission!* Kashe clan was a group of unique creatures with the ability to manipulate energy. They could control energy through tiny slits in the palms of their hands. Some Kashe used their abilities to help. Others liked to blast defenseless beings just because they could. The Kashe council had spoken out against the rogue group. She grinned, remembering Amethyst's encounter with the band of miscreants two years ago. Even though the group could wield power stronger than a blaster, Amethyst had made quick work of them when they attempted to lord their abilities over the Agonahan people.

"They call themselves Zoran now, to distinguish themselves from Kashe. They believe they are superior and should dominate their quadrant of the galaxy."

"Zoran, huh? So what do they want with the Sullarians?"

"If you ask me, they are just pushing the Sullarians around to get attention. Unfortunately for them, it's the wrong kind if we're on their radar."

"If they want a round two, we're ready."

Lewis smiled. "I thought you would say that. We're meeting with Commander Stewart now."

***

Commander Stewart, Nova, and Morris were already seated at the conference table when Ember and Lewis walked in. She didn't miss the ripple of surprise in Stewart's eyes as she claimed her seat.

"Agent Wilson, this is a private meeting."

"Yes, with Amethyst." She nodded.

He ran a finger under the collar of his shirt, as if the material was suddenly strangling him. "Ember . . ."

"I am still a member of this team, Commander."

"I thought we discussed this."

"Wilson is our leader," Morris spoke up. "We won't take on any mission without her."

Pride swelled in her chest as Nova and Lewis nodded in agreement. The Commander didn't look moved.

"But she —"

"Is just as capable as she was six months ago," Lewis cut him off. "She's still one of the finest agents the ISC has ever known."

"I know, but —"

"Are you seriously standing against us, Commander?" Nova squared his shoulders back and narrowed his eyes.

Stewart swallowed hard. "Fine. Welcome to the meeting."

Ember looked at Nova out of the corner of her eye and he winked. Stewart always backed down anytime any member from Amethyst stood up to him. He took a moment to compose himself before he began.

"All right, so this is what we know. The Kashe have asked us to help with a rogue group calling themselves the Zoran. The miscreant group has targeted a farming colony on Sullalore. The Kashe leader, Golker, has asked for Amethyst specifically, since you handled them without causalities a couple of years ago."

"That was fun," Nova said with a grin.

"Any clue as to why the Zoran would target the Sullarians?" Morris asked.

"Sullarians farm the dungal fruit, which is the Kashe's primary food source. We believe they are sending a message," Stewart explained.

"Starving their own people? That's low."

"Which is why we're going to stop them," Ember said.

"I don't need to tell you to be careful. We have a good relationship with the Kashe and we don't want it to be ruined by the Zoran."

"We hear you, Commander," Lewis said.

The quartet stepped away from the table. She was barely out the door when she heard the Commander's voice speak to someone still in the room.

"Watch her out there. Don't get her get hurt."

"Ember isn't weak. I think she'll surprise you."

She didn't need sensitive hearing to be able to listen to the conversation between Stewart and Lewis.

"Don't let your feelings overshadow your good judgment."

"Emmitt, cut the crap. This is Ember we're talking about. She'll be great."

"For her sake and yours, I hope you're right."

***

Ember quickly walked to the armory to collect weaponry and prepare. Nova and Morris were already filling their bags with energy food packs and smoke grenades when she came in. She pulled her bag off of the hook on the wall and began gathering her stuff.

"Hi, guys. I wanted to thank you for what you said back there," she said. "You'll never know how much it means to me."

"Aw, no sweat, Wilson." Nova pulled a pack of gum from his front shirt pocket and popped a stick into his mouth.

"You would do the same for any of us," Morris said as he attached his belt around his waist.

Lewis wouldn't meet her gaze when he entered. He sat down without saying a word, running a hand through his hair.

"Here." He held up a small metal bracelet.

She looked at him curiously and accepted it. The metal was cool in her hand and had a slight blue tint to it. Two tiny buttons were in between the ISC logo engraved in the center. She growled when she recognized it, throwing it back in his face.

"You've got to be kidding me."

"Having a personal shield on this mission is more than a safety protocol. It's necessary."

"Yeah? Are you wearing one?"

He blanched. "No."

"Then why should I?"

"Because my body can absorb shots from the Zoran and yours can't."

He blurted out the words without thinking. It was evident on his face he meant what he said, but he instantly regretted how he worded it. She recoiled away from him. Nova wrapped an arm around her shoulder, bringing her close to his side. Morris stepped protectively in front of them with his arms folded over his chest.

"Come on, guys. I'm just looking out for her."

"Yeah, and so are we," Nova said.

"You've trained with her. You know what she can do," Morris growled.

"I know." Lewis sighed. "I just want to be careful."

"We watch each other's backs," Morris insisted. "We always have. Nothing has changed."

"It's okay." She stepped out of Nova's embrace and lightly touched Morris's shoulder. "Guys, I really appreciate the show of support, but it'll be okay."

"Can you placate me by wearing it, even if you don't activate it?"

Lewis held up the bracelet again. She fumed and snatched it from his fingers.

"Fine. But I'm not happy about this."

"Duly noted."

CHAPTER TWELVE

It took a week for Amethyst to fly out to the Sullarian system. Ember had managed to grade the papers and had been happy to pass all of her students. The rest of her time had been split between watching the holonet and playing an advanced role playing game. She caught Nova online shopping for engagement rings. Lewis had been playing a long distance poker game with several of the guys from the Luteus team, a group of pumpkin-eyed sharpshooters.

By the time the ship dropped out of hyperspace, Ember was already searching for a new game to play, Nova was showing off a holo of the ring he bought, and Lewis was gloating over his poker win.

"I've got visual," Morris announced.

Ember walked over and stood behind his pilot's chair as the planet came into view. It was probably half the size of Earth, and due to the distance away from the solar system's sun, it was usually thirty degrees colder, even in the warmest spots. The Sullarians grew most of their crops underground to protect them from frost. Both the Sullarians and the Kashe were a vegetarian race. Their primary food source, the dungal, was a sweet, large red berry. It amazed Ember how they were able to come up with so many different ways to prepare the fruit.

Everyone put on their thick coats and grabbed their gear. Ember placed her hood over her head to protect against the freezing wind. She was grateful for the wool gloves as she slipped them on her hands.

"All right, we take the Zoran down, but no kill shots," Ember instructed. "Use the smoke grenades to blind them. Our blasters will be pretty useless, but they won't be any match for our physical strength. Subdue and capture. Protect the Sullarians."

Morris set their ship into standard orbit above the planet and the quartet beamed down. A blast of cold wind blew through her coat. She shivered as she tightened it around her, but the material didn't feel like it did much good against the elements. Nova, Morris, and Lewis didn't look nearly as affected by the weather as she did, and it annoyed her.

The Kashe were tall, slender beings who seemed to radiate light. Due to the energy they absorbed and controlled, they always had a glow about them. Their skin was nearly translucent. Their leader had long, silvery hair. He was the only one Ember had seen with hair. The Sullarians were the opposite. The tallest stopped at her knee. Nova called them rock trolls and it wasn't far from the truth. They were stocky and their skin was hard, like stone. Most of the younger ones preferred to roll instead of walk.

Snow crunched under their feet as they walked in a flanking formation toward a village. A translucent being covered in an orange glow stood at the center of the village. There were three other beings standing behind him with the same orange glow. Cowering at their feet were several Sullarians. The leader looked at the foursome, his lips curling into a snarl.

"Ember Wilson. What brings you here?"

"Detak," she began, recognizing him. "You know why I'm here."

"So the council sent you to deal with us. They couldn't do the dirty work themselves."

"You will let the Sullarians go."

Detak laughed. "You have no authority here. Be gone while you still have legs to stand on."

"You remember the last time you engaged us in a fight?"

"So kind of you to remember the past. But I had anticipated the council sending you." He stretched his arms out to the side and the orange glow grew brighter. "And this time we're prepared."

"Give it your best shot," she challenged.

The Sullarians rolled out of the way as Detak began his approach. They burrowed under the snow, but Ember could still see their eyes peeking out. Nova and Morris spread out, moving to engage two of the Zoran clan behind their leader. Detak's hands began to glow before an energy ball shot toward her. She leaped to the side and rolled forward, springing up to her feet. Her fingers slipped underneath her glove on her left hand, pressing the two tiny buttons on the bracelet to activate the protective shield. She dodged a punch meant for her head when she felt a tingle over her body, hovering over her skin. She could hear a low hum in her ear and instantly realized her mistake.

The shield used a low energy pulse to guard against attacks. Under normal circumstances, it would protect her. But to an enemy who could *control* energy? It meant she had given him an additional weapon.

She attempted to kick Detak, but his reflexes were faster than hers. He caught her leg and his eyes lit up as he felt the shield running over her body. He grasped under her thigh and squeezed. Pain flooded her system and she cried out.

"Ember!" She heard Lewis's voice cry out for her.

Detak smiled and turned his wrist, using the shield he now had control over to flip her. She landed on her back, air rushing out of her lungs. She couldn't move as the pain increased. Suddenly, her body felt as if it were on fire as sparks emitted from Detak's hold on her leg. It was hot. Too hot. He stood over her with a satisfied smile on his face.

"I'm going to enjoy this."

She couldn't help it. She screamed as the pain intensified. It felt like someone was standing on her chest, making breathing nearly impossible. Her entire body shook uncontrollably. Her heart raced faster than she had ever felt it before, and there was nothing she could do.

And then everything went black.

***

A new kind of pain awoke her. Ember's eyes fluttered open and she gasped for breath. Relief temporarily washed over her once she could breathe without struggle. Then the pain returned. It felt like a sonic hammer was pounding inside her head. She could move her fingers and toes, but the rest of her limbs felt heavy. She swallowed hard, wincing at the raw feeling in her throat. Her eyes floated around the room to get acclimated to her surroundings.

She was back in the hospital wing of the ISC. Her entire body felt stiff. When she looked down, she could see why. A thin, white cloth was covering her arms and legs. It was how the medical staff treated burns. The skin under the cloth itched and tingled - signs it was healing. She closed her eyes and breathed deeply. A short, stabbing pain radiated from her ribs, and she groaned.

"Hello, dear," a sweet feminine voice softly greeted. "We weren't expecting you to be awake so soon."

Ember slowly opened her eyes to see a tall, blonde woman standing at the foot of her hospital bed with a tablet in her hands. She wore mint green scrubs with cartoon characters covering it. She smiled sweetly as she approached Ember's right side.

"I'm Sidney Prowess, your nurse. How do you feel?"

Ember grimaced and the nurse gave her a short nod.

"I'm sorry, forgive the question. I know you probably feel like the transporter malfunctioned upon cellular reconfiguration. We're required to ask."

Sidney pulled a small tray table from the corner over to the bed. She helped Ember sit up and positioned the pillows for comfort. The nurse handed Ember a cup of water.

"Thank you," she said before sipping eagerly.

"You are a very lucky girl. We had to put you in a medical coma, but you kept waking up! You finally complied and we were able to work on fixing you up."

"What happened?"

"You had second degree burns covering your body except for your face and neck. Two of your ribs were broken and your left thigh muscles were ruptured."

"That makes me lucky?"

"You could've been dead."

"Well, there's always tomorrow."

Sidney gave her a plastic smile and wrote her vitals down on the data tablet she had in her hands.

"I'll let you rest and let Dr. Grace know you are awake."

If Ember could've raised an eyebrow right then, she would've. "Dr. Grace?"

"Dr. Peyton Grace." Sidney brushed away strands of blonde hair from her eyes. The smile was still there but Ember could see the lines around her eyes harden. "And don't make that face. Dr. Grace is fantastic."

"I'm sorry."

"It's quite all right."

Ember sighed as the nurse swept out of the room. She stared at the cracks in the ceiling until they started to blur together. After thirty minutes, there was a soft rap at her door.

"Yeah?"

The door swung open and another tall blonde came in. The woman had a long white coat over her navy blue scrubs. She gave Ember a reassuring smile before tapping on the screen of her tablet.

"Hello, Agent Wilson. I am Dr. Grace. It's good to see you're awake, but I must say, I am baffled as to why."

"Why I'm awake?"

"Yes. You see, we had a hard time keeping you under a medical coma."

"So I've heard. If you couldn't keep me under then, why are you baffled now?"

"Anyone with your injuries should be asleep for at least a week while healing. They would also be in an extreme amount of pain when they awoke. You, however, seem to be doing fine. Do you have a high threshold of pain?"

"Evidently. My head is pounding, if that makes you feel better."

Dr. Grace flashed another courteous smile. "It's not about me, Agent Wilson."

"You know what I mean, Doc."

"How are you feeling?"

"Like a planet has landed on me."

"That's understandable. I'll have Nurse Prowess give you something for your headache."

Dr. Grace walked to her side and pressed into her rib cage. Pain shot through her body the instant there was pressure. Ember sucked in a sharp breath and pulled away.

"Sorry, but I have to check. I thought you had a high pain threshold?"

"Not when you jab already-broken ribs, Doc."

Dr. Grace chuckled. "You're going to be difficult, aren't you?"

"Pretty high-handed talk."

"Suppose I should be grateful you haven't punched me yet."

Ember smirked. "What makes you say that?"

"The look in your eyes. It's not hard to figure out."

"I like you, Doc." Ember relaxed into her pillow and closed her eyes. "Go ahead with your exam."

This time the contact wasn't as painful. Ember didn't complain as her ribs were checked.

"You're healing nicely and you should have very little issues."

"You sound surprised."

"A good surprise. The amount of abuse your body endured before your crew put you in a med tank was astounding. I'm happy to see you are responding so well to treatment. Do you feel up to visitors? You've had an anxious young man waiting for you."

Lewis. Ember looked down at the white cloth covering her arms and ran her teeth across her bottom lip. She let go of her lip and nodded. Lewis had seen her in worse shape than this before.

Dr. Grace left, and Nurse Sidney Prowess appeared with a syringe in her hand.

"Your headache should go away in a few minutes," she said as she injected the needle into Ember's temple.

"Thanks." Ember closed her eyes again and sighed deeply.

She was right. The headache started to dissipate quickly. Ember reached over and grabbed a cup of water and gave the nurse a thankful smile.

"Your boyfriend looked mighty relieved when I told him you were awake."

"I don't have a boyfriend."

"Well, whatever you call him. He wouldn't leave even when we told him it would be a while. I saw him sleep in the waiting room. Pretty handsome, too. I should probably tell you I asked if he wanted to come home with me, but he wouldn't leave your side."

"Mighty forward of you to tell me you hit on him."

"Guess I should just let you know I think you're lucky to have a man like him."

"Well, like I said, he's not with me."

"Hmm. . . Not sure if he knows that."

"Believe me, he does."

There was a glimmer of something in the pretty nurse's eyes that Ember didn't understand. Jealousy? Resentment? Dismay? She was used to seeing that look from people, but never when it came to a man.

"Is there something you want to say?" Ember asked.

"Nothing. It's not my place to question why you would act so aloof when it comes to a man like that."

Ember narrowed her eyes. "No, it's not. And I'm not dismissive toward Lewis."

Sidney looked confused. "Who?"

"Michael Lewis." Ember blinked a few times when Sidney failed to respond. "The man in the waiting room."

"Isn't Lewis."

It wasn't Sidney who spoke. Ember froze, her heart skipping a beat for a moment. The monitor next to her started to beep loudly before shutting off. Her eyes swung to the foot of her bed to see Liam Ross holding a single red rose. He wore a wrinkled, gray shirt and had stains on his blue jeans. Liam's black hair hung down into his eyes, and he hadn't shaved in several days. Relief filled his eyes as he looked at her.

"Hi, Ember."

"Hi, Liam."

She stared at him for a moment before looking over at Sidney.

"You're still here. Change it."

Sidney's cheeks turned red and she bowed out of the room. Liam and Ember stared at each other for several tense moments before she broke the silence.

"Liam, what are you doing here?"

"Your father told me what happened. I transported here immediately."

"Why?"

"Why?" Liam shook his head and put the rose down on the food tray next to him. "You are really thick sometimes."

"No, I mean." She sighed. "We didn't leave off on the best of terms last time you were here."

"I know. It's been weighing heavily on me and I wanted to apologize."

Ember was stunned. *Apologize to me? But I am the one who acted out of line.*

"I should've been more understanding of what you were going through. I should've known better than to push you as hard as I was."

"I wasn't exactly fair to you, either."

"Does it matter?" Liam shrugged. "I think you were justified."

"I was hard on you."

"No, you pushed me away." He walked over to the side of her bed, pulled up a chair, and sat down.

"You didn't want me to be around, and I think I know why."

"Liam . . ."

"I'm not asking for anything. I'm not making grand promises to be here for you or declarations of love. I know how much you hate that mushy stuff. I just wanted you to know I came as soon as I heard you were hurt."

She smiled appreciatively at him. She tentatively reached for him and he took her hand in his and pressed it to her cheek.

"I just . . . wanted you to know."

"I know. And thank you, Liam. It means more than you know."

He looked relieved and gave her hand a gentle squeeze. After a moment, he paused and reluctantly let her go as he stood up.

"I guess I should be going then."

He had taken two steps toward the door before she called out to him. He stopped and turned around.

"Would you stay with me until I fall asleep?"

"Of course."

He settled down in the chair again. She settled down under the thin hospital covers. Liam brushed some hair off of her forehead and she closed her eyes.

"I like the blonde, by the way."

She smiled sleepily. "Going back natural."

"Are you starting over?"

"Sure feels that way," she muttered.

She heard him speak, but couldn't focus on his words as she drifted off.

Chapter Thirteen

Disappointment filled her when she woke up to an empty room. She wondered if he had been a figment of her imagination until she saw the rose sitting in a vase next to her bed. Liam really had been there. His simple gesture warmed her heart.

She had been in the hospital for a week to fully recover before Dr. Grace signed the release. During the week, the only other visitor she had was her father, who she spoke with through video chats since he couldn't leave Washington, even if it was by transport.

At first, she was hurt. No one in Amethyst had visited or sent get well wishes. The more she thought about it, the angrier she got. As soon as she was released, she asked the computer for Lewis's location.

"Michael Lewis is in Conference Room C."

He must be getting ready for a mission, she thought. She took off for the conference room, storming into the meeting.

"Agent Wilson!" Commander Stewart exclaimed as she barged in.

"Can it," she snapped at him before turning her attention to Lewis. "What the hell?"

"Look, I'm sorry!" Lewis scrambled away from the conference table. "We felt it was best —"

"*We*? Who is we? You and this figurehead of a commander?"

"Now see here." The Commander stood up.

"I said shut up!" she bellowed. The color drained from his face and the Commander sat down in his chair.

"Not Commander Stewart," Lewis said. "Nova, Morris, and I."

His words stabbed her in the heart. Ember faltered and stared at him, her mouth agape.

"The three of us thought it would be best. You could heal on your own terms and not feel like you were rushed to rejoin us."

"The three of you," her voice drifted off.

"Yes. Ember, I am sorry. I know what you must be thinking —"

"You mean like I've been abandoned?"

"We would never abandon you!"

"My team didn't check on me. My team didn't visit me!"

"We're not your team anymore! That mission proved it."

It felt like someone had a vice grip on her throat and was slowly choking the air out of her. The room began to blur. Ember had to grip the table to keep herself steady.

"We're not abandoning you."

"Aren't you?" She managed to keep her voice steady as she looked up. Three of Lewis's heads floated in her line of vision but she focused on the middle one. "All that talk of supporting me was just talk."

"No, it wasn't."

"Then what was it?"

"It was the truth! But the situation has changed."

Something inside of her twisted at his words. She sucked in a deep breath and her vision cleared. She narrowed her eyes and clenched her fists in anger.

"The situation didn't change. You knew my condition before we left Earth. You admitted it, but vouched for me. You trained with me so you knew what I was capable of. You whispered encouraging words in my ear when I took you into my bed. You even made me wear the shield! Why was that, Lewis? When we were going against an enemy who could control energy, why make me activate a device to have electricity run over my entire body?"

He winced at her accusations but he didn't respond.

"You have no excuse! You might as well have placed me in that hospital bed!"

"You're right," his voice was barely above a whisper.

"What was that?"

"I said you are right. It was my fault. It was my failure, and it nearly cost you everything. That's why we stayed away. We all felt responsible. We didn't know what to say to you."

"And now?"

"It's apparent to us that even with our abilities, we can't protect you."

"I don't need protecting!"

"Yes, you did. A normal mission, maybe not. But Amethyst doesn't go on normal missions, Wilson. We undertake ones no one else can handle. No matter how hard you train, or how hard you push your body, you will always be in danger with us."

"And you are all in agreement?"

"Yes." Lewis nodded.

Commander Stewart cleared his throat. Ember swung her gaze over to him. The man looked petrified as he addressed her.

"Until we can sort out your situation, you're on a leave of absence."

"My situation?"

"Until we can find a proper ISC team —"

"A proper ISC team? Are we not still researching to duplicate the Genesis Project?"

The Commander and Lewis exchanged looks. Ember crossed her arms over her chest.

Ember threw her hands up in exasperation. "You've got to be kidding me."

"You're a hell of an asset even without Amethyst and I can't risk losing you," Stewart said.

"Can you duplicate the Genesis Project?"

"No."

"Are you going to try?"

"No."

"And you've been lying to me?"

"I had been hoping you would give it up and relent."

"No chance." She shook her head.

"I see this now."

Her eyes burned into his until Commander Stewart was forced to look away. "Go to hell. Both of you."

***

She wasn't surprised when Lewis didn't follow her out of the conference room. There weren't any cries for her when she turned and left the room. No one stopped her in the hallway. Commander Stewart might be a liar, but he wasn't dumb. She didn't need to have purple blood in her veins to take down a few security guards if any were to approach her.

The door for her apartment slid closed silently behind her. The rooms felt emptier than usual. She rummaged through the bottom of her closet to find a bag full of civilian clothes and tossed it on the bed, dumping its contents out. She left her ISC uniform on the floor and slipped on a pair of comfortable jeans and a long sleeved shirt. Ember grabbed the amethyst necklace Liam had given her from her nightstand and fastened the chain around her neck. She pulled a suitcase from under her bed and filled it with clothes. The bag was refilled with some of her favorite weapons. She surveyed her room, frowning at the blank walls. She reached into the side pouch of her suitcase and pulled out the handheld holo projector. The small device fit in the palm of her hand. She flattened her hand out and pressed the button on the side. It opened up and a small light projected the image of her family. It was a photograph taken when she was little. She looked to be around eight years old. Her sister, Laura, stood beside her, beaming up at the camera. Ember looked at her smiling parents standing behind the two girls. The familiar pain stabbed her heart as she looked at her mother. It was the only image of her that Ember had. They looked like one happy family.

Maybe the three of us can be again, Ember wondered.

She shut the photographic image off and placed the device back in her suitcase pouch. Ember removed her wrist communicator and threw it on the bed. She quickly recorded a message of resignation on her tablet and put it on the bed next to the device.

She didn't look back as she grabbed her two bags and headed toward the transporter pads. Thankfully, there wasn't a wait. The transporter room at the ISC looked like any other transporter room. Clean white walls and ceilings. Light pads could hold up to six grown men in a circle. The only other equipment in the room was the control panel operated by a man who looked bored out of his mind. Ember always wondered why they had a person manning the transporters. It was simple to operate and there hadn't been a transporter malfunction in over a hundred years. A technician looked up as she entered.

"Evenin'," the technician nodded toward her, his voice heavy in a West Virginian drawl. "Where are ya headed?"

"Washington, D.C."

"Any wheres in particulars or want me to dump you in the middle of the city?"

"Do you know where the terminal is nearest the Felix squadron barracks?"

"Felix, eh? Yeah, I can get you there."

"Thanks."

She stepped up on the transporter pads and nodded toward him.

"If ya don't mind me sayin' so, Miss, it looks like you runnin' from somthin'."

"Not running from," she corrected. "Running *to* some*one*."

"Good to hear." He grinned. "All right, Miss. You're good. Enjoy."

Ember closed her eyes as a bright light filled the pads. The hair on the back of her neck stood on end as a warmth rolled over her skin. The room dropped away and her stomach momentarily flipped before settling back down. She opened her eyes to see the exact same room she was just in but with a different technician. She nodded and stepped off the teleporter pads. She left the transporter room and stepped out on the busy streets of D. C. It took her a moment to get her bearings before she walked over to the barracks.

Her father had told her previously where Liam's quarters were. A smile tugged on the corner of her mouth, mentally thanking him for sticking his nose into her business. She paused when she reached his door, hesitating for a moment before knocking.

The door opened and a surprised Liam stared agape at her. At least he looked like he had gotten some rest. He was freshly shaven and had gotten a haircut.

"Ember! What are you doing here?"

"I'm here for you. For us, actually."

Before she could say another word, Liam wrapped his arms around her slender waist and pulled her to him. His mouth covered hers and she dropped her bags so she could wrap her arms around his neck. He pulled her inside, breaking his embrace long enough to toss her bags in and shut the door behind them.

Chapter Fourteen

It was the most content Ember could remember feeling in a long time. She awoke in his arms, smiling into his skin. His heartbeat counted the seconds as she laid with him, soaking in the feeling. He stirred, pulling her out of her bliss.

"I still can't believe you're here," he said as he rubbed his thumb over her shoulder.

She nestled against him, her head resting on his shoulder. She reached over and traced the outline of his muscles on his stomach, grinning when she saw goose bumps form.

"I can leave if you want."

"I keep expecting this was a dream and you'll disappear."

"Do you still feel me in your arms?"

"Yes."

"Against your skin?"

"Ember, you're under my skin."

She poked him under the ribs. "I'm not going to disappear."

"I hope not. I'm just happy you're here."

His lips brushed against her temple. She breathed in his scent, letting the smell of his skin fill her. She drifted off to sleep peacefully in his arms.

When she awoke, she was startled to find she was alone in the bed. The smell of bacon filled the air. She grinned and kicked back the covers. She didn't break her stride as she picked up one of his shirts off of the floor and put it on.

Liam was standing at his stove, wearing nothing but his boxers as he fried bacon and eggs. A stack of pancakes was on a plate on the counter. Rock music blared from his sound system and he was singing under his breath. She grinned as she watched him dance at the stove.

"Morning," she greeted.

He jumped and gave a startled cry. She covered her mouth to keep from laughing as he spun around, nearly splashing bacon grease on him.

"Ember, you nearly gave me a heart attack!"

"I'm told I have that effect on men. Honestly, who were you expecting?"

He took the bacon and eggs off the burners and reached her in two strides. His arms wrapped around her as their lips met. He pressed his forehead against hers after they broke their kiss.

"You look good in my shirt. Damn good."

"And you look good wearing nothing, but isn't that dangerous? What if you got burned?"

He chuckled as he looked into her eyes and rubbed her arms. "Not much of a cook, are you?"

"Why cook when you have access to a mess hall and replicators?"

"Because nothing tastes as good as something from your own kitchen."

"I'll take your word for it."

Liam motioned for her to sit down at his kitchen table. She gave him a sideways look and sat in one of the wooden chairs.

"You've got a nice place. It's much better than my small dorm," she said.

"Perks of being a major. How did you know I was here?"

"I have my ways."

"Ah. Tell General Blanchard I said hi."

She was about to say something, but her words were cut off as he approached with two plates. She breathed in the heavenly smell of bacon and pancakes. The rich aroma of coffee filled the air and she licked her lips.

"And this is real coffee. None of that instant stuff," he said as he placed a cup in front of her.

A small pitcher of warm syrup was placed on the table and he sat down next to her. They ate in silence for several minutes.

"Liam, this is fantastic. Thank you."

"Of course. I actually like to cook. And it's nice to have someone to cook for."

She had just finished her eggs when she noticed Liam watching her. She ignored him and ate her pancakes. The fork dinged against the plate when she dropped it.

"What are you staring at so hard?"

"Are we going to talk about it?"

She leaned back in her chair. "What's there to talk about?" He gave her a hard look and she sighed.

"Couldn't let us get through breakfast, could you?"

"Come on, Ember. Talk to me."

"All right. The short version is I went out on a mission and got hurt. You were the only visitor I had. So, me being me, I barged into a meeting between Lewis and Stewart who told me I was relieved of my duties and he wasn't going to help me get back what I lost. So, I left."

"That's the short version?"

"Condensed. Cliff notes, as it were."

"Lewis didn't stick up for you?"

"That's the long version." Ember picked up her last piece of bacon and let it drop back on the plate. "No, he didn't. He said I was someone he needed to protect. Basically called me a liability."

"I find that hard to believe."

"Lewis looked me in the eyes and said I wasn't the leader of Amethyst anymore. I would be a great agent on normal missions, but they don't go on normal missions."

"Wow." Liam's shoulders slumped as he leaned back in his chair. "That's harsh."

"Can't really say he's wrong though."

"Ember, purple eyes or blue. Blonde hair or black. It doesn't matter. No one can deny you are the toughest woman in the ISC."

"Yeah, well, I'm not in the ISC anymore."

"So because you can't go through the process again, you don't want to be a part of it?"

"I don't want to work under a commander who is going to lie to me and try to manipulate me to get his way."

"Fair enough. So what are you going to do now?"

"I haven't figured that out yet."

"Well, whatever you want to do, you have my support. And you can stay here as long as you'd like."

"Thanks. I appreciate it."

He almost looked sheepish as he reached out and held her hand. She gave his a gentle squeeze and pulled back.

"For a moment there, I was worried there was still something going on between you and Lewis."

She paused momentarily. "There was."

"He acted like he loves you."

"That's what he said."

"And you?" His eyes met hers.

"I'm here, aren't I?"

"But are you here because you want to be or because of what happened?"

"What would you do if I answered the latter?" She crossed her arms over her chest and angled her body to look at him better. "Would you make me leave? Would you turn me away?"

"No." He shook his head. "I just need to know how much I have to guard my heart."

His eyes were pleading with her for an answer. She saw hope, love, and a little fear. Her heart swelled as she looked at him. She leaned over, positioning her face so she was inches away from his.

"I want you to understand something," warmth filled her voice as they locked eyes. "I am here because I want to be. You've been on my mind since the moment you left. I know what you want to hear, and believe me, I feel it, but I can't say it."

"Why? Why are those words so hard for you?"

"They just are. It's . . . giving up control."

"I know you are a control freak but telling me you love me doesn't give me power over you."

"Yes, it does. Right now, I can protect myself. If something were to happen, it would hurt, but I would be guarded. If I gave you my heart —"

"Then I would promise never to break it. Ember, I would go to the ends of the known galaxy for you."

"I know, and I hope you know I feel the same way. Can't this be enough for now? Could you be happy with me not saying the words, but knowing it is how I feel?"

Her words hung in the air for several moments. He gazed at her with his jaw set before smiling.

"You drive me mad, Ember. Being with you makes me happy. So, yes, even though I think you're being silly, I would stay with you forever if you'll have me."

"You mean it?"

"Of course I do! I love you, Ember."

"Same here."

Liam chuckled. "Then I guess that's settled."

"Guess so."

He smiled as he shook his head. Liam reached for her plate, but Ember smacked his hand. "But that doesn't mean you get to eat my bacon."

***

They spent the next few hours wrapped up in each other before Liam had to leave. Ember watched from the bed as he put on his Air Force blues.

"It's taking every ounce of will power to drag me out of this room," he said. "Get back quickly."

"Oh, I assure you, I will."

She lay back in the bed, feeling content with the world for a change. Ember couldn't remember a time when she felt more at peace and happy. She didn't know what the future held or what she was going to do, but it didn't matter. The future was going to come regardless. No sense in ruining her good mood thinking about it.

She resisted the urge to go through Liam's personal belongings. She didn't think he would mind if she did. It just seemed wrong to do so, considering her personal effects were some clothes and weapons. She studied the photos on the wall. In one picture, a teenage Liam was standing next to an older man who bore a striking resemblance to him. The older man also wore an Air Force uniform. Ember was able to make out the name Ross on his name badge. As she looked at the photo, she realized she didn't really know a lot about Liam. She didn't know what his parents' names were, if they were still alive, or where he grew up. Judging by the photos on the wall, he had an older brother and younger sister. The thought also popped in her head that he didn't really know her either.

Could you love someone you don't really know? The thought alone was painful. She pushed it aside, trying not to dwell on the impeding thoughts. She settled on the couch and watched entertainment programs while counting down the hours until Liam came home.

"Ember!" His voice called from the front door as he entered that evening. "In here!"

Liam was unbuttoning his blue shirt as he entered the living room and grinned.

"You must've been bored all day to watch a musical."

She looked over at the screen and shrugged. "I like them."

"Do you? I wouldn't have thought."

"Are you kidding? Imagine a time where there wasn't any health care. Disease ran rampant. The government and military was corrupt. The people were starving. All they had were these ancient weapons. Then a ragtag group tried to take a stand against a heavily outmatched force. It's inspiring."

"If I recall correctly, didn't they all die?"

"They wouldn't have if I had been in charge."

He smiled. "I don't doubt that, Ember."

"How was your day?"

"Pretty good. Doesn't compare to my evening though."

He sat down on the couch next to her, draping an arm around her shoulders. She leaned against him and sighed.

"Are you hungry?" he asked. "What would you like for dinner?"

"Let's order in," she suggested. "I don't want you to have to cook and we don't have to use the replicator if you don't want to. But let's just stay in and talk."

"Talk?" He raised an eyebrow.

"Get to know one another."

"What do you mean? We know each other."

"No, not really. We've fought alongside each other and have shared a bed, but there is still lots we don't know."

"What kind of stuff?"

"Real things. Personal stuff. I tell you my sins and you can sharpen the knife."

Liam laughed. "I think you're more comfortable with knives than I am."

"True, but I think you know what I mean."

"Yeah, I know what you mean. All right, let's talk."

Food was delivered from a Chinese place Liam favored. They sat on the couch eating their food from the cartons and began to open up to each other.

"I have an older brother named Marcus," Liam began. "He is an engineer with the ISC. My little sister, Millie, is three years younger than me. She's a florist."

"A florist?"

"She loves it. I don't get it either." Liam shrugged. "Whatever makes her happy. My mom is a successful baker. She's where I get my love for cooking." His thumb rubbed her shoulder. "I have a confession to make."

Ember looked at him warily. "What's that?"

"My father was in the Air Force. He's actually old buddies with your dad. So I've actually known General Blanchard for a long time. He was a huge influence in my life. He talked fondly about his daughter. He even went as far as suggest she and I go out on a date. Although," Liam scratched his chin. "He didn't really mention you. He never mentioned a legal name, but he often talked about his princess."

"That's Laura," she reminded him. "My father took exception when I resigned my commission for the ISC. We had a huge fight after I underwent the Genesis transformation. We didn't speak again until I went to him for help regarding Dr. Clayton Rudo's plans."

"And he dismissed you."

"You know the story. It's what eventually led us here."

"Can't say that part was good, but the rest has been."

Ember's happy expression became more somber. "I think that's a matter of opinion."

"I know you aren't thrilled with what happened regarding the croceus poison, but it did turn out okay. You're here, aren't you?"

"Yes. Yeah, you're right."

"The past sucks, but it is the past."

"Yeah. So your dad knew mine?" Ember was eager to change the subject. "You grew up in Washington?"

"For the most part, yeah. Spent a majority of holidays and summers in Wilmington, North Carolina as well. Your dad was really there for me when mine died."

Ember managed to push aside the familiar jab of jealousy. It seemed like her father had been there for everyone but her. She could feel the usual ball of resentment grow. Liam looked at her oddly.

"What's that look for? I thought you were getting along with your dad?"

"Yeah, now, for the most part. I have even gotten to the point where I could have a real conversation with him without threatening injury. That doesn't atone for the past."

"He loves you, Ember. Don't lose sight of that."

"Maybe he does now."

"No, he's always loved you."

"You can't tell me that. You just said you've known my father for many years and he never mentioned me."

"Well, that's true, but a parent loves their child."

"How did your dad die?" She blurted the question out.

Pain registered in Liam's eyes before he answered. "He died defending the science station orbiting Jupiter."

"I am so sorry."

"Thanks. He died a hero, though."

They fell silent for several moments. Liam shuffled in his spot on the couch, tapping his foot on the floor. Ember sucked in her bottom lip and glanced up at the ceiling.

"Well, this is becoming depressing," she said.

"Think we've talked enough?"

"Absolutely."

Liam pounced on her, pinning her shoulders down. She laughed as she reached up to kiss him.

Chapter Fifteen

It was a week before anyone from the agency reached out to Ember. She was mildly surprised and annoyed by the lack of response to her departure from the ISC. However, if she and Liam had taken bets on who would've contacted her first, she would've lost. The image of an angry Lewis appeared when she answered the call.

"You left?" She could visualize smoke coming out of his ears as he glared at the screen. "You fucking left the ISC? And for what? Him? Have you lost your fucking mind?"

"Michael . . ."

"No! You left, Ember. You walked away! Don't talk to me all calm and rationally."

"Will you shut up a moment?"

Her tone caught his attention. He huffed but nodded.

"I am not going to be a part of something that's a lie. Commander Stewart had no intention on helping me. He just wanted to manipulate the situation to fit his needs."

"Come off it. You're not dumb. It's not like the commander intended for this to happen."

"And what steps have been done to correct it? What has happened other than a million sorries?"

"So what if you're not purple anymore? You were a part of this —"

"No, I wasn't. I resigned my Air Force commission to be a part of the Genesis Project. I was never truly a part of the ISC, Lewis. None of us were."

"You could've stayed —"

"No, I couldn't. There is nothing left there for me."

"There's me."

She paused and looked at the screen warily.

"Don't give me that, Ember. We're good together. No, scratch that. We're great. And you know it. You're just so scared of having real feelings, afraid it would show vulnerability. But you forget I've seen you at your most vulnerable. I carried you. Been there for you."

"Abandoned me."

"No, I didn't," he hotly said. "Distance isn't abandoning."

"Do I need to remind you of what you said?"

"No, I remember my words. And God knows I wish I could take it all back. I've been choking on them every day for a week now. But leaving like you did." He shook his head. "You're better than that."

"I'm forging ahead. I'm starting over. It took walking away from that life to create a new one."

"Are you sure it's worth having? I mean, he may be good with a blaster, but Ross isn't strong enough to handle you."

"Liam is part of the equation, but he isn't the whole picture. Besides, he's been *handling* me pretty well."

Something twisted in his face momentarily. She recognized a mixture of pain and sadness before he peered stoically at her.

"I know he has feelings for you, but no one is going to love you like I do. And no one is going to be a better family than Morris and Nova."

"I never disputed my family."

"No, I suppose you never have. But you do dispute my claim."

She wasn't sure how to answer him. She couldn't deny their physical connection, but was it more than that? Could they have been more if she had allowed herself to be open to the possibility? She pushed the thought away. She never wanted more with him. Being with Lewis was a release. It was comfortable and fun, but there wasn't anything real behind it. At least, that was what she kept telling herself. Looking into his eyes then, she wasn't so sure of herself.

"I don't know," she finally replied, speaking as honestly as she could. "But I'm here now."

"Yeah." Lewis slowly nodded. "I can see that."

"Tell Morris and Nova to call me sometime, okay?"

"I will. Ember?"

"Yeah, Michael?"

"Tell Ross if he's not good to you, I'm going to teleport there myself and beat his brains in."

She grinned. "I will."

***

Ember wasn't surprised when the video alert sounded several minutes later. The image of Morris and Nova shoving each other into position to share the comm for the transmission made her smile.

"Knock it off," she sternly said.

"Hi, Wilson," Nova said, grinning as he loudly chewed on a piece of gum. "You look good."

"Thanks. How are things?"

"Wish I could say same as usual, but nothing has been the same since you left."

"Good to know I'm missed."

"Of course you are." Morris snorted. "Didn't think we'd forget about you so easily, did you?"

"Nah, Wilson is unforgettable. Even if you bump your head."

"Thanks, Nova. Miss you guys."

"So you aren't still pissed at us?"

"Not really. Irritated is a better word to use."

"Good," Nova said, still grinning. "I can take you being irritated at us."

"Yeah, that's par for the course." Morris laughed.

"Har har. You guys are hysterical."

"Are you enjoying your break?" Morris asked.

"Break?"

"Yeah, Lewis said you're on a break."

"Oh, he did." She pressed her lips into a thin line.

Morris punched Nova in the shoulder. "I told you she left."

"Ah, hell, Wilson. What did you leave for?" Nova asked as he rubbed his shoulder.

"Because Commander Stewart wasn't going to help me duplicate the Genesis Project. And I'm not going to have my crew looking at me like I am a liability. Not going to happen."

Both men appeared uncomfortable. "Did Lewis say that?" Nova asked.

"Something along those lines."

"Can I go on record and say I don't agree with that and he didn't speak for all of us?"

"He says he did."

"I promise you he didn't."

"So noted."

Nova shoved Morris hard enough to knock him completely out of the frame. Ember heard him crash on the floor and yell but he didn't immediately pop back up.

"So you're back with Ross?" Nova asked.

"Yeah, I'm at his place in Washington."

"Good." Nova's purple eyes shined brightly at her. "I have my money on you two."

Nova yelled as he was pushed out of view. Another loud crash made Ember cover her mouth to keep from laughing.

They always fought like brothers. Morris ran a hand through his black hair and grinned.

"He's wrong. The money is on you and Lewis." Morris winked. "But we've got to go. See ya!"

He waved at her and then the transmission ended.

***

"I hope you won't get mad, but I've arranged for us to have dinner this week with your dad and sister," Liam said as they sat down for dinner.

Ember groaned. "Are you serious? Why?"

"Because they are your family and you've been here for over a week now. I don't even think Laura knows you're here."

"And you're sure we can't keep it that way?"

"Honestly, I'm surprised at you. I would've thought after all that's happened, you would want to mend the bridge there."

"I do." Ember stabbed at the piece of steak on her plate. "I was just hoping for a little more time before I get bombarded by Air Force Barbie."

Liam laughed. "She's not so bad."

"Says the guy who was going to date her."

"I was never going to date her. It was your father who wanted me to."

"Ah, that's the distinction."

"An important one."

They fell silent for several moments. Ember poured them a glass of wine. Liam finished cutting up his steak.

"So are we going to talk about your conversation with Lewis?"

Ember stared agape at him for a moment. Liam wiped his mouth and grabbed a dinner roll.

"I get the transmission transcripts to my digital box, Ember."

"Right." She nodded. "Well, then you know. Nothing else to talk about."

"Isn't there?"

She glanced at him over her wine glass. He stared hard at her as he chewed a piece of steak.

"I need you to let me know if I have to fight for you. Because I will, if it comes down to it."

"Fight for me? What the hell are you talking about?"

"You said you didn't know. Why?"

"Oh, for crying out --!" She growled and pushed the plate away. "What do you want from me, Liam?"

"I want you! I've always wanted you."

"You have me!"

"Yeah, sure. I have the part of you that you want me to have. But you seem content to have me your way and keep me at arm's length for everything else. I want all of you. Heart, body, and soul."

"You have it." Her voice had grown soft. It sounded eerily quiet to her. Her hands began to tremble as she looked at him.

"I don't wear my emotions on my sleeve. I don't cry or giggle or draw hearts on things. I don't skip around the apartment singing songs, and I don't use the l-word. But I have opened myself up to you in ways I haven't with another human being in a very long time. I don't share how I feel well, but I was hoping you could see it in my eyes. The only way I know how to express it is by my touch. I'm guarded to a fault. I recognize that. The chip on my shoulder has dug into my skin more times than I care to count. But I'm only myself when I'm with you. Liam, I promise you, I am happy. You do have all of me. Every broken piece is in your hands."

"Oh, Ember. You're not broken."

She broke away from his gaze, unable to meet his eyes.

"Aren't I? I get defensive if someone gets too close because I've lost too many people in my life. A few I've managed to get back, but I still can't completely forgive my father. I want to, but I don't think I have that kind of forgiveness inside. I look in the mirror and I don't see myself. I see my mother. Sometimes it makes me smile to see her. And sometimes it makes me angry she's not here."

"That's a natural reaction. My father died protecting the base. I am proud to be his son and the choice he made, but I'm angry he's not here, too. But it's okay to talk about it."

"What difference does it make? You can't change the past. The ISC outlawed time travel."

"I'll make a deal with you." Liam reached across the table and took her hands in his. "If you promise to show more of yourself to me, I promise I won't tell the world how incredibly sweet and loving you are."

Ember made a face. "I doubt anyone would believe you."

"Just don't hide yourself from me. I'm the one person you don't have to."

"I promise."

***

She was thankful Liam didn't push the issue with Lewis. Frankly, she was tired of thinking about it. She wanted a day of peace with him, only he had to mess it up with dinner plans with her father and sister.

Ember came out of the sonic shower and begrudgingly got dressed. She didn't have much in the way of nice clothes, so she requested a dress from the replicator to her measurements. She stepped in front of the mirror to examine herself. The purple garment hugged her curves nicely, but didn't overly flaunt her figure. The hem of the dress stopped above her knee. The scoop neckline showed off the amethyst stone Liam had given her from the caves of the Maulians. Her blonde hair was pinned up away from her face with several silver pins and she let it cascade down her shoulders. She stepped into a pair of black pumps and grimaced over the pinching in her toes.

"Women actually walk around in these?"

Liam came up from behind her and wrapped his arms around her waist.

"Yeah, and some even like it."

"Sadists."

She looked herself up and down and frowned.

"What's wrong?"

"I have no place to hide a weapon."

"Ember, we're going to dinner."

"Hmm . . . You're right. I could probably strap a small blaster to the inside of my thigh."

Liam spun her around and tilted her chin up for her to meet his eyes.

"You look beautiful. Now relax."

She took a deep breath and nodded. He kissed the tip of her nose before briefly touching her lips.

"Come on, it's going to be great."

She grumbled over his enthusiasm. He smiled as he offered her his hand and they left the apartment.

The warm breeze hit her as soon as they stepped out into the night air. The sidewalks were lined with couples enjoying the first warm day in months.

"I swear, wasn't it just winter?" Ember asked.

"You've been in isolation for a while." Liam squeezed her hand. "We haven't had snow in a few weeks."

"Really?"

"Now that the ISC has Dr. Rudo's weather machine successfully working, it's like clockwork now."

"Seems rather boring."

"You would prefer the unpredictable weather?"

"I prefer a natural order to things."

As soon as the words left her mouth, the irony of what she said washed over her. She covered her face with her hand and Liam laughed.

"Yeah, I heard it as soon as I said it."

"Just as long as you're aware."

Liam opened the door for her at the restaurant. The hostess showed them to their table where her father and sister were already seated. Her father rose and smiled as they approached.

"Wow, Ember. You do look . . . so glad you could come."

"Thank you for having us."

The general looked over at Liam and the two men shook hands. Ember felt uncomfortable as Liam held out the chair for her. They sat down and placed a drink order. Laura flipped her long hair over her shoulder. She reached over and stroked his forearm.

"Well, hello. It's good to see you again," Laura purred, batting her eyes at Liam.

"Keep it in your pants," Ember snapped, smacking Laura's arm away.

Laura turned her attention to her sister for the first time, glaring. "You're one to talk."

"Ladies," their father sternly said. "Enough bickering."

Laura looked smugly at her sister. Ember rolled her eyes.

"Princess, what have you been up to?"

"Well, Daddy, I started taking up skiing lessons," Laura joyously said.

"Skiing lessons?" Ember dryly asked.

"You can never have enough outdoor sports." Laura squared her shoulders back and tilted her nose up in the air.

"Be careful you don't get a nose bleed, Your Highness."

"Ember, I thought I said no bickering," her father snapped.

Ember grumbled under her breath and picked up the menu. She could see Laura looking complacent over the top of the paper. Liam placed a hand on her knee and gave it a squeeze.

"So, anyway, yes, I'm skiing now. My instructor, Jean Paul, says I have real talent."

"I bet," Ember said under her breath.

Liam squeezed her knee again and she sighed. She wrinkled up her nose and tried to let go of the annoyance building.

"You caused quite a stir, leaving the way you did," her father commented as he buttered a roll.

Ember shrugged. "My business."

"I'm not going to lecture you. It's your life. I would just caution you on burning bridges."

"That's not something I want to be a part of."

"Would you feel this way if you could be a part of Amethyst again?"

"Of course not. I would love to walk back through those doors with Amethyst."

"What would you do to accomplish your goal?"

"Just about anything. Why do you ask?"

"Just hypothetical talk."

Ember raised an eyebrow and paused. The waiter came by to take their order. The conversation was dropped. She sipped on a glass of wine, listening as Laura prattled on about her new ski instructor and her latest modeling commercial.

"So they wanted me to dress up as this scientist to advertise some sort of new medicine. I don't know. Anyhoo, they actually had a real scientist on set to show me how to do things. He was real nice although not very attractive. Still, perhaps I should call Dr. Fergas."

"Dr. Fergas?" Ember leaned forward in her chair, suddenly very interested in what her sister was saying.

"Yeah, Dr. Timothy Fergas. Think I should go on a date with him? I mean, I could do worse than a scientist, right?"

"I don't care about that. Did he mention if he's still working with the ISC or not?"

"I'm not sure. Do you know him?"

"As a matter of fact, I do."

"You're kidding." Laura's eyes lit up. "I wish I had known. Then I would've had something to talk to him about."

"Do you still have his number?"

"Yeah, but why would you want it? Aren't you with someone?" She looked sideways at Liam.

"Not for a date. I have a favor to ask him."

"Yeah, I can give it to you after dinner."

Ember reached across the table and grabbed Laura by the wrists and squeezed.

"What the hell, Ember? I told you I'd give you the number."

"It's important, Laura."

"Okay, okay."

Ember released her hold. Laura rubbed her wrists and looked sourly at her. She pulled a piece of paper out of her bag and handed it to her.

"Thank you! You don't know how much this means to me."

"What's this about?" Liam asked.

"I'll tell you later." She turned to the general and leaned forward. "You asked what I would do to get back into Amethyst." He nodded. "Why did you ask? Was it more than hypothetical?"

"Yes."

"Do you know something?"

"Yes. I was going to call, and then Liam invited me for dinner." He grinned and wiped his mouth with a cloth napkin before winking at her. "Let's just say the meeting between Dr. Fergas and Laura was no accident."

Liam looked confused. "I don't understand."

"Dr. Fergas was the scientist in charge of the Genesis Project," Ember explained. "And it'll be him who helps me duplicate it."

CHAPTER SIXTEEN

Ember was practically skipping as they left the restaurant. *Dr. Fergas! He is the missing puzzle piece to finally get the process started.*

"You know there is no guarantee this will work," Liam said.

"Never tell me the odds."

"I'm just saying to be realistic."

She glared at him but didn't say anything. Liam wrapped his arm around her waist and leaned his head on her shoulder as they walked. She shrugged him off, but the smile never dropped off her face.

"I know what I'm up against. Believe me, my eyes are wide open in this. I'm not looking at this with rose-colored glasses. Trust me, all right? Yes, I am excited and eager, but that doesn't mean I have lost sight of the dangers."

"I hope not." Liam frowned.

"I appreciate your worry."

"Of course I'm worried," he scoffed. "I'm not exactly bursting with joy over the fact the woman I love is rushing off into a dangerous situation."

"Aww, you're cute when you act all tough and defensive."

"Don't brush me off, Ember."

"Liam, relax. Let's hear what the good doctor has to say before you get your panties in a bunch."

"Fair enough."

They hastily walked back to Liam's apartment. Ember strode directly to his monitor and placed a video call. Within seconds, the smiling face of Dr. Timothy Fergas appeared.

"Hello again, Agent Wilson."

"Dr. Fergas." She bowed her head in respect.

"You look different than last we met."

"How much do you know?"

"More than you, I'd assume."

"Tell me something I don't know."

"It's best if we talk in person. I'll be at your door in five minutes."

The transmission ended. Ember leaned back in her chair and sighed. Liam rubbed the tension out of her shoulders.

"I'm not sure who is more nervous about what Dr. Fergas has to say," she commented.

"I can answer that. Not sure if you want me to though."

She smacked his hands away. "Please don't make this more difficult than it has to be."

"I'm just nervous, all right?"

She turned around and studied his face. Something in his eyes made her nervous.

"Liam, what aren't you telling me?"

He broke eye contact at her question. The hair on the back of her neck stood on end.

"You're planning something."

Her voice was accusatory. He closed his eyes and shook his head.

"You are, aren't you? You're planning something you don't want me to be a part of."

"Not entirely true."

"Which part?"

"I think it's best if we wait for Dr. Fergas," he said.

Her eyes narrowed and she opened her mouth to argue, but the door chime cut her off. "Saved by the bell," she said as she brushed past him.

She pressed her thumb against the door plank and it slid open. Dr. Fergas was a tall and thin man with thin metal glasses sitting on top of his short nose. His dark hair was longer than when she had last seen him, now having grown past his ears. He grinned and extended his hand.

"So much nicer to speak in person," he said.

She shook his hand. "Dr. Fergas, thank you for coming."

She stepped aside so he could enter. Dr. Fergas nodded at Liam.

"Major Liam Ross, I would presume?"

"Yes, sir."

"Pleased to finally meet you. General Blanchard speaks very highly."

Ember raised her eyebrow but didn't comment. The scientist looked around the apartment before grinning.

"Nice place you have here."

"Thank you," Liam said.

Ember walked over to the kitchen table and pulled out two chairs for both men to join her. Dr. Fergas set a bag on the floor with a heavy thud before taking a seat. Ember folded her hands in front of her on the table and gave him an anxious smile.

"I believe you were going to enlighten me."

"All in due time. I believe social protocol would have you offering me something to drink. A coffee, perhaps?"

"Fine." Ember clenched her teeth as her irritation rose. "Would you like some coffee?"

"No thanks, I'm good." He waved her off.

She dragged her teeth across her top lip. He had always been an eccentric man.

"I know you are anxious for us to begin. You must have questions."

"Tons. Let's start with, what did you mean earlier by knowing more than I do?"

"Ah, yes. It's best to start from the beginning. I've always felt like a proud father to those who made it through the Genesis transformation. Amethyst was my crowning jewel. Because of that, I have kept close tabs on you and your team. Naturally, when you were injured several months ago, I was concerned."

"So you know the medical facts."

"Of course. But here is where I get to drop the first bit of knowledge on you."

He bent down and picked up his bag, placing it on the table with a loud thud. He pulled out a vial filled with a yellow substance.

"This is a sample of your blood with the croceus poison," he explained.

"You kept it?"

"I had to study it. I have most of this tainted blood back in my lab. The croceus infiltrated every cell, which had been filled with the amethyst formula, and destroyed it, leaving this in its wake. At the time, the doctor felt the transfusion had been the only course of action that would've saved your life. The decision was made to carry it out."

"I know this."

"Yes, you do. But I've been able to run successful tests on this, and I believe I have a way to improve your current condition."

"Improve?" Liam interjected. "Improve how?"

"Because of how her body reacted, the medical doctor believed it was killing her. However, it behaved similarly to the amethyst formula."

"By eradicating the previous cells," Ember slowly said.

"Exactly!"

"Are you saying Ember would've survived if the doctor had left her alone?" Liam asked.

"She would've been changed, but yes. Well, yes and no."

"Yes and no?"

"My tests of her yellow blood proved to be on par with the amethyst formula. She wouldn't have been purple, but she would've kept her increased abilities."

"So where does the 'no' come into play?" Ember asked.

"That's the tricky part. It would've come with a price. The croceus is highly volatile. It's possible you would've been extremely aggressive and uncontrollable."

"Just what the world needs," Liam joked.

Ember gave him a sideways glance before smiling. "So it would've killed me."

"Potentially. You may have been able to maintain your abilities, but the stress it would've put on your system makes me doubtful."

"But you said you have a means of being able to improve?"

"Through my testing, I have come up with two methods to assist you. One way would be to use a smaller amount of croceus in hopes it won't turn against you. The second option actually incurs a slight change to the original amethyst formula."

"How slight a change?"

"Hard to say. You could experience elevated levels in strength and dexterity. Or you could be slightly below your previous scores, but still above your current abilities."

He spoke casually, as if he was talking about the weather. He smiled cheerfully at Ember and she imagined crushing his head against the table. Instead, she gave him a plastic smile.

"So with the croceus formula, she could be better than she was before?" Liam questioned.

"Oh, I would say definitely yes."

"But we can't say for sure how her body will react."

"Oh, my dear boy, I can't say for sure how her body would react to the amethyst formula for a second time either."

"Either way, I could die," Ember said.

"There are always risks with science, Agent Wilson. It's up to you if it's worth it."

"It is to me. How soon can we get started with the amethyst formula?"

"Not even going to consider the croceus?"

"No, I don't trust it. No offense, Dr. Fergas, but you didn't go through what I did. I don't think I could hand my body over to it again, even if you could guarantee my survival."

"I suppose I understand that. Are you sure you want to undergo the procedure again?"

"If you can do it, yes."

"My tests have all been hypothetical. I haven't been able to create the formula yet."

"I understand. What do you need from me?"

"This is where it gets tricky." Dr. Fergas leaned back in his chair. "I am missing two ingredients to successfully create the formula again. One will be easy to get. I need a small sample of pluchiot from the Agonahan homeworld."

"Pluchiot?" Liam asked.

"It's a power source. We need something strong in order to act as a catalyst."

"That's incredibly simple. We could almost send a scout team to get it," Ember said.

"You could, but you pass by the Agonahan planet on your way to the second ingredient," Dr. Fergas said.

"Where's that?"

"Agent Wilson, are you familiar with the Oda?"

She grimaced. "More than I care to be."

"What's an Oda?" Liam asked.

"They are the residents of the Kolick planet. The Oda don't have a skeletal system."

Liam made a face. "Seriously?"

"They are green, slimy beings that look more like a dessert flan than creatures. You can't fight them and they have regenerative powers, so any blaster fire is ineffective," she explained.

"She's right, but it's also where the mines are for the amethyst dust," Dr. Fergas said.

"And they don't like outsiders. They are mean, hostile creatures. If they get too close, they will attempt to absorb you," Ember said.

"Absorb?"

"Anything organic can be a part of their diet. They have the ability to swallow a man whole and let him digest in their stomach. It's a little reptile-like, but far more disgusting."

"Sounds like a terrible way to die."

"Can you think of a good way to die?"

"Hopefully as an old man and warm in my bed."

She tried to keep a straight face, but the gleam in his eyes made her smile. She cleared her throat and looked away, regaining her composure.

"How much of the amethyst dust would you need?" she asked.

"Two pounds should be sufficient for our needs, but I do have a request."

Of course he wouldn't do this without a fee. "What kind of request?"

"Once you go through the transformation, I need you to recover a device for me."

"What kind of device?"

"It's a time device."

"No." Ember shook her head. "Time travel is outlawed centuries ago by the ISC for a reason."

"This is special. The device was created by Dr. Mackenzie Rhodes."

"So? Just because it was made before the ISC banned traveling through time doesn't change anything," Liam said.

"Don't refuse so hastily," Dr. Fergas warned. "When the ISC placed a law on the practice, any equipment created for the use of traveling through time was placed in a stronghold to ensure they didn't fall into the wrong hands. Most of them have been kept in the ISC under security protocols, but Commander Pulaski thought it was perilous to have all of the devices under one roof."

"Commander Pulaski? That was fifteen years ago," Ember commented.

"Indeed. This device was placed in a security locker under the surface of an uninhabited world. I want you to get it for me."

"You want Amethyst to be your delivery boys?" Ember raised an eyebrow.

"I would create a dummy device to put in its place. No one can know the actual device has been moved."

"No." Liam shook his head. "Absolutely not. Time travel is risky, Doctor."

"I have no plans on changing history, Major Ross. Just consider me an aficionado of Dr. Rhodes."

"You expect us to believe this is going to sit on your shelf like a trophy?"

"More or less." He grinned, but there was no humor in his smile. "The device is precarious, and if it fell in the wrong hands, it could spell disaster for the galaxy."

"So you are looking out for the universe's best interest and not personal gains," Liam said, his voice flat.

"Well, if I gain a few extra gold bars, no one would be the wiser." He shrugged.

Ember and Liam looked at each other, trying to gauge the other's reaction. She could see the distrust he had for Dr. Fergas in his eyes. She didn't trust him, either.

"If we do this, then I have two conditions," Liam said, turning his attention back to the scientist. Dr. Fergas' lip twitched. "Such as?"

"We will retrieve the device, but we keep the power source."

"Unheard of!" Dr. Fergas raised his voice.

"So is a scientist trying to supersede his very organization's rules."

"I told you, I wasn't going to use the device to alter the past or the future."

"If that's the case, then our condition wouldn't be a problem," Ember pointed out. "Unless you would like to take this matter up with Commander Stewart?"

Ember managed to hide her smile as she watched his disposition change. He knew he had been cornered.

"That won't be necessary," Dr. Fergas said through clenched teeth. "What is your second condition, Major Ross?"

"Ember won't be the only one to go through the Genesis Project. I want to undergo the process as well."

CHAPTER SEVENTEEN

"Have you lost your fucking mind?"

Liam winced at Ember's angry words. He couldn't blame her reaction. He had debated several times talking to her about the decision he had made, but he had been afraid of her reaction. Now he faced her full wrath for springing this on her.

After he dropped his little bombshell, Ember grabbed him by the collar and pulled him out of the kitchen. He followed her into the bedroom and let her explode.

She paced furiously around in the bedroom as he sat quietly on the bed.

"Answer me! Have you lost your fucking mind?"

"I think we need to take a moment and calm down."

"You calm down! I am calm."

"Ember, please."

"How long have you been planning this?"

"Ember —"

"How long, Liam?"

He sighed. "Since you came here."

She reared back and punched him in the jaw. Liam groaned and dropped back on the bed. Tears welled up in his eyes as pain moved through his face. He held his jaw as he rolled back into a seated position. Ember's eyes burned with fury.

"Lewis is right. You are an ass. So what's your big plan, huh? Fill my head with lies so you can worm your way into the program?"

"Fill your head . . . What the hell are you talking about?"

"Oh, you're all talk!" she ranted. "All this talk about love and how everything will be great as long as we are together. What a load of crap!"

"That's not true! I have meant everything I said."

"Then what is this?"

"I told you I wanted to be with you in every facet of your life. And that includes Amethyst."

He watched as his words stunned her. The anger dropped off her face and she sat down on the bed next to him. She took his hand in hers and looked deep into his eyes.

"Liam, I want you just as you are. You don't have to change to make me happy."

"I know, and it's not why I want to go through this. You told me when you left the Air Force for the Genesis Project, every aspect of your life changed. I can only imagine the adventures you embarked on. Everything you've seen, all that you've done, is the stuff of legends. I want to be a part of it too."

"You don't have to go through the procedure to come along."

"Don't I? Lewis is content to throw my inferiority in my face every chance he gets."

"Who cares what Lewis says?"

"I know how much this means to you. It's more than the benefits of Amethyst. It shines in your eyes, regardless of its color. I want to be a part of this with you, Ember."

"Liam, it's dangerous."

"Everything we do is dangerous. I know the risks, same as you."

"So all the talk earlier about being careful . . ."

"I'm not going to lie and say I'm not scared. Only a fool wouldn't be. There is a reason genetic manipulation isn't commonplace. But, like you, I think it's worth the risk."

She looked at him long and hard for several moments before shaking her head and smiling.

"You really are an idiot."

A huge smile appeared on his face. He knew her well enough to know that her statement was her way of conceding. He wrapped his arms around her as his lips crashed down onto hers. She pressed into him, thrusting her hands into his air. The sound of someone clearing their throat made them pull apart. Liam looked up to see Dr. Fergas leaning in the doorway with a smile on his face.

"Sorry to interrupt, but if we are going to do this, we really should get started."

"Right." Ember cleared her throat, quickly regaining her composure. "Well, if we're going to Kolick, we're going to need to assemble a team."

"Right. Wouldn't be smart to go just the two of us."

"Let's go get the band back together."

***

"Do you realize how insane you sound?" Nova asked in disbelief after Ember and Liam explained the situation. "Don't get me wrong, no one wants you back more than I do, but we barely escaped with our skins the last time we visited the Oda."

"I'm aware," Ember said. "But I'm going. It's up to you if you're coming with me or not."

"Well, of course we're coming with you!" he scoffed. "I just wanted to point out you're crazy."

"Of course she's crazy," Morris chimed in. "There's no guarantee it'll work."

"It'll work all right," Lewis said. "What other choice is there?"

"Death," Nova gravely said.

"There's always that," Morris said.

"Yeah, but this is Wilson we're talking about. I don't think even death would stop her," Lewis said.

Ember leaned back in her chair and kicked her feet up on the table. She looked over at Liam and winked. The other three men continued their discussion as if she wasn't in the room.

"Don't mistake me. Like I said, I'm all on board for getting her back, but the Oda will be guarding the mines," Nova said.

"I'm not that worried about the Oda," Lewis commented.

"Not worried about the Oda? Since when?"

"Since there are other pressing matters."

"Ah, you mean like Dr. Freda asking for a time device?"

"That's Dr. Fergas and yes."

"I don't see what the big deal is. Ross already told him we would take out the power supply and he agreed."

"Agreed a little too quickly, it sounds like. I have a hard time believing he would go through the trouble of asking us to retrieve this thing for it to sit on his shelf."

"I don't know. There are stories of the great lengths archeologists took to get their hands on relics that once belonged Dr. Rhodes and Dr. Brooks," Morris chimed in.

"Archeologists centuries ago," Lewis argued. "And this isn't an ordinary relic."

"True, but if we don't get this thing, he won't help Wilson."

"Do we know that for certain? He can't back out if he's already done the process."

"I don't trust him. He still has the croceus liquid, right? How do we know he won't do something to her with it or to any of us for that matter?"

"Fair point."

Ember cleared her throat and the three men turned to look at her. Nova turned bright red while Morris and Lewis looked unabashed at her.

"Sorry, Wilson," Nova sheepishly said. "Kinda forgot you and Ross were there."

"No harm done," Liam assured him.

"What do you say, guys? Feel like going out on an adventure?" she asked.

"I say hell yeah," Morris replied.

"I vote yes," Nova said.

"Of course." Lewis nodded. "Always."

Liam growled at Lewis's words. Ember grabbed his forearm and squeezed.

"Not now," she whispered.

"No, I want to hear what Major Tight-pants has to say. Go on, pretty boy," Lewis goaded.

Liam shook his head. "Ember's right. Now isn't the time for our squabbles."

"Yeah, but soon it'll be an even playing field. Assuming you survive, of course. And when that day comes, we're going to settle this once and for all."

"Looking forward to it."

Chapter Eighteen

Ember could feel the tension radiating between Lewis and Liam as she sat between them on the ship. Nova and Morris sat in their pilot chairs, chatting. They seemed obvious to the silence in the flight chairs.

"I'm telling you, you need to check out the program," Nova said. "They don't make holo shows like that. Did you know that Dr. Mackenzie Rhodes, Dr. Madison Brooks, and their families appeared on an episode? Yep, it was right after they defeated the Synth."

"No, can't say I knew that. Of course they don't make programs like that anymore. That's why it's in the archives. What's the name of the show again?"

"Pay attention. It's called *Doctor Who*."

"And he's a time traveler?"

"He's a time lord. I swear, you never pay attention."

"I do so, but often times I think you like to hear yourself talk."

"Now that's just hurtful."

Ember smirked at their banter. Lewis sighed and leaned his head back against his chair.

"Do you two do anything else other than bicker? You sound like an old married couple."

"Aww, was that a teensy bit of jealousy in your voice?" Nova asked.

"Sounds like it," Morris agreed.

"Think it's because the good major stole his woman?"

"In order to have stolen something, it would've had to have been his in the first place," Liam said.

"I would recommend keeping your mouth shut about matters you know nothing about, or I will do it for you," Lewis responded.

"Enough!" Ember threw her arms in the air. She unfastened her seatbelt and stood up so she could see both of them. "I am so sick of this. Both of you need to knock this off."

Both men glared at each other. Lewis crossed his arms over his chest and narrowed his eyes. Liam squared his shoulders back, looking ready for a fight.

"I am not playing around. Stop this at once," she insisted. "Or I will personally see to it that you won't get laid for a *really* long time, Liam. And I will promise you that you won't want to sleep with anyone for a very long time once I'm done kicking your ass, Lewis."

Liam and Lewis both looked down at the floor. Neither of them seemed to be able to meet her gaze. She crossed her arms over her chest and glared at them. Several moments went by before she heard one of them speak.

"You're right. I'm sorry," Liam said.

She waited for Lewis to reply, but he remained silent. She knew him well enough to know he wouldn't apologize. Instead, he looked up at her with determination burning in his eyes. She squared her shoulders back, as if answering his challenge.

"We're approaching the planet, Wilson," Nova alerted her.

"Drop us out of hyperdrive and engage in orbit above the planet."

"Aye."

They beamed down several moments later. Ember had always liked the Agonahan homeworld. It was very similar to Earth, only everything was miniature in stature. The Agonahans were a race of tiny beings, the size of an Earth eight-year-old, but were very advanced for their position in the galaxy. Ember looked over at the capital city with its small buildings and vehicles which floated several inches from the ground. She always felt like a giant when she visited there.

They had beamed outside of the Agonahans biggest city on the little planet to avoid any destruction of the buildings. The planet's inhabitants had created a building centuries ago for visitors in a field nearby. She could see a hover car speeding in their direction. It came to a stop several yards from them. Ember smiled and bowed her head as she recognized the leader, Balian, approach. She had always liked Balian. He had a calm, yet strong demeanor one would expect from a leader. He stood several inches taller than the other males in his race. He had long, brown hair, which he kept in a braid, and big, round brown eyes.

"It's good to see you again," she greeted.

"The pleasure is mine, Ember. Always good to see you and your team." Balian spoke in a high pitched voice. "Although your physical appearance differs from my last memory."

"I've been through some changes. Looking to get back what I lost."

"I see. And you've come for help."

"If you could."

"Certainly. However, I am concerned as to why you came unannounced. Normally a visit from the ISC starts with a formal declaration from your agency."

"No one knows we're here."

His eyes widened. "Is everything all right?"

"Yes, everything within the ISC is functioning normally. Except for me."

"I see. What can I do to help?"

"I need a small sample of pluchiot."

"You know the pluchiot is not a toy to play with."

"We aren't going to do anything dangerous. My partner and I," she motioned toward Liam, "need it to fuel the machine to undergo the change."

"Ah." His eyes swung over to Liam. He looked him up and down before grinning. "He appears to be a good partner for you. I'll be happy to assist."

She didn't miss the scowl on Lewis's face over Balian's comments. She managed to swallow her smile and she poked Liam in between the ribs when she saw his smirk.

Balian motioned for them to follow him into the tall building. It had been designed over a thousand years ago as a meeting place for other races. The stone had lost most of its luster, but it was easy to imagine it was once a beautiful place.

The team walked through a narrow hallway in single file until it opened up into a large meeting room. Ember and Balian stood at the head of a long, wooden table in the center of the room while the others sat down.

"How much do you need?" Balian asked.

"Two drops," she replied.

"Seriously? Two drops? That's all we need?" Nova questioned.

"The pluchiot is a power source beyond your world," Balian stiffly said. "Not much is actually needed."

"Two drops will be sufficient for us," Ember reiterated.

She pulled out a glass test tube she had in her pocket and handed it to Balian. The container, which fit perfectly in her pocket, nearly engulfed Balian's hand. He studied it before shaking his head.

"The pluchiot is stronger than this glass. I will have something fortified for you."

He walked over to a row of cabinets lining the floor against a wall, the door creaking as he swung it open. He rifled through the contents, muttering under his breath. Ember heard the sound of glass clinking together before Balian made a happy squeaking noise. Nova began to laugh, but one look from Ember silenced him.

"This will do much better," Balian stated as he shut the cabinet door. "I shall be right back."

Ember had her eyes locked on Nova as the leader left the room. As soon as he was out of earshot, Nova burst out into a laughing fit.

"Stop it at once!" Ember admonished.

"I'm sorry, but didn't you hear that noise? He sounded like a squeaker toy."

"Nova, Balian is the leader of a brilliant and noble race."

"Who happens to sound like Morris when he inhales helium."

Morris punched Nova in the shoulder. "I don't sound like that." He squared his shoulders back and stuck out his chest. "I still sound manly."

"Does a chipmunk sound manly?"

"You two really sound like an old married couple," Lewis said. "Why don't you two go consummate?"

"Not into that." Morris shook his head. "I have a woman."

Nova looked mildly surprised. "Seriously?"

"I told you I date."

"Yeah, but I didn't think you were serious. Is this Trisha?"

"Lila."

"Ah, yes. Beeka told me about Lila."

"Seriously, you guys can go into the back of the ship if you need to. I can take the helm when we need to take off," Lewis said.

"Hey, I'm not gay. Not that there's anything wrong with that," Nova said. "But even if I was, I could do better than him."

"Yeah, right. You should be so lucky," Morris said. "I'm a catch."

Ember shook her head, unable to remove the smile from her face. She had really missed them.

Balian returned a few minutes later with a proud grin across his face. He presented Ember with a vial no bigger than a thimble.

"Two drops, as requested."

"Thank you, my friend."

"Be very careful. This is sealed for protection, but that doesn't mean you shouldn't exercise caution."

"I understand. I appreciate your assistance."

"Certainly. Is there anything else I can help you with?"

"No, this is more than enough."

"Come visit us again when you're not on official duty."

"I will."

Ember and Balian respectfully bowed their heads to one another before the team exited the building. Ember waved goodbye and then activated the transport module on her wrist. The team transported back to their ship.

***

If only their next was as easy.

Ember placed the container with the pluchiot in a security hold as they made their way toward the planet Kolick. Tension hung in the air the closer they got to the planet.

"I have a question," Liam's voice cut through the quiet. "If the Oda don't have a skeletal system, how do they mine?"

"You really want to know?" Ember asked. Liam nodded. "They use the amethyst dust several ways. All involves absorbing."

"So they swallow it?"

"In a matter of speaking. They are coated in a slimy substance. They are able to stick on walls."

"Yeah, it's kinda neat if it's not on your face," Nova said. "Watch them scale the walls, I mean. Not the absorption. That's always gross."

"They really are foul, mean creatures," Morris said.

"I'm sure the same could be said for us," Lewis said.

"Yeah, but do you fart purple dust into storage containers? We don't," Nova said.

Ember smiled and shook her head. Liam looked horrified at the description.

"Kolick used to be the home of an advanced species thousands of years ago, or so the legend states," Ember informed.

"What species?" Liam asked.

"No one knows. The name has been lost from the database. But history states that a once mighty empire lived here. There was a huge volcano in the center of the planet. When it erupted, it killed every living thing and buried the civilization. Over time, the volcanic rocks cooled and began to form amethyst mines."

"Supposedly, the Oda rose from the ash," Morris said. "Hard to believe those horrible, slimy creatures are on the same planet as the substance that gives us our abilities."

"Science gives us the abilities," Ember corrected. "Amethyst is fuel."

"My point remains valid."

The systems started to alert them they were getting close to the planet. Nova dropped them safely out of hyperspace and into standard orbit above the planet. Liam looked out the screen, surveying the strange planet. It appeared almost dead from space. It seemed nearly black, but Liam could swear he saw a purple tint in the atmosphere. He wasn't sure if it was his imagination or not.

"All right, everyone know the drill?" Ember asked as she passed out the blasters. "No physical contact with the Oda. Make sure setting number three is on the blasters."

Liam looked over his blaster and adjusted the setting. The third option wasn't one he used often. The first two settings were stun and kill. The third was to electrify. It wouldn't kill, but it might be enough to keep the Oda at bay long enough if the team fell under attack.

Ember zipped up her jacket and grabbed a saber hanging from the wall in the storage locker and tied the hilt to her hip.

"What's that for?" Liam asked.

"In case one of us gets swallowed. The sword won't kill the Oda, but it will let me open up a hole big enough to pull the victim out before digestion."

Liam grimaced. "How fast does digestion start?"

"Start? Instantaneously. How much time would we have to save one of us? Matter of moments."

Nova and Liam tucked the containers for the purple dust under their arms. The team gathered around in a circle and then activated their transporters. A white light engulfed them and they quickly disappeared. A chill was in the air and there was a faint smell of iron surrounding them. The ground crunched under their boots as they walked toward a mine several yards in front of them.

"I never understood why the transporter couldn't just plop us down right next to it," Nova complained. "I don't like being out in the open like this."

"You know why. The transporter could cause tremors which would alert the Oda to our presence," Morris explained. "Beaming down away from the caverns reduces the risk."

There weren't any structures around them other than the mines ahead. No trees to use as shield. Liam swallowed the fear he felt beginning to swell inside him.

"Where ... where do the Oda live?" he asked, trying to distract himself. "I don't see anything other than the mines."

"That's where they live," Morris answered. "That, and in

the   —"

"Ground!" Ember shouted, finishing his sentence. She pulled Liam out of the way as a green arm burst through the dirt and reached for his ankle.

The team fanned out with their blasters at the ready. Lewis shot the arm. There was a cry from the surface as it became electrified and it withdrew into the dirt. Several green blobs began to emerge from the earth. They moaned in unison as they bobbed their way toward the team.

"Run!" Ember yelled, firing her blaster toward one.

The men ran off without a second glance. Ember fired two more shots before following after them. Liam looked back over his shoulder to make sure she was all right, but she shouted at him.

"Don't worry about me! Just get the dust!"

Nova and Morris stopped at the first mine they came to. Lewis shoved Liam forward.

"Next one is ours," he barked.

More Oda appeared along their path. Liam set to work on gathering the dust as soon as they were at the mouth of the mine. It was coarser than he had expected. He scooped dust from the walls and began filling his container. Moans from deep in the mine began to echo until they thundered in Liam's ears.

"Hurry it up!" Lewis ordered as he fired his blaster at an Oda reaching for Liam's arm.

One of the creatures moved on the wall, sliding over to them. It dropped down, but Liam saw it in time and moved before it landed on him. He rolled out of the way, making sure his container with the dust came with him. He snapped the lid on and quickly got on his feet. Ember looked inside the mine.

"Did you get enough?" she asked.

"It's full."

"Good. I want you to beam back to the ship."

"Without you? No way."

She fired her blaster right above his head, stunning an Oda who was getting ready to drop.

"No time to argue. Get back."

The sound of Morris yelling made their heads snap around. The three of them raced out of their mine toward the other two men. Morris was surrounded by several Oda with the container at his feet. Ember gasped in horror. Nova was inside one of them. Lewis and Liam started opening fire and she pulled out her sword.

"Nova, hang on!"

His face was pressed against the gelatin body, looking like he was screaming without any sound. Ember sliced off the Oda's arms and began hacking away at the side.

"Duck!" she yelled.

His hands covered his head and he moved down as far as he could conceivably go. She sliced right above where his head was. Green slime splattered on the ground and began to bob its way back to the main body. This time, Nova's screams were loud and clear. She stuck her sword into the enemy again.

"Liam, get the hell out of here!"

Liam managed to tear his eyes away from the horrifying scene to fill the second container as quickly as he could. More Oda seemed to appear out of nowhere. Lewis grabbed the second container and activated his transporter, beaming back to the ship. Morris ran over to stand back-to-back with Liam, helping Ember fend off their enemy as she worked desperately to free Nova. He looked over to see Nova begin to climb out of the creature, and moved to help.

"Grab my arm!"

Nova accepted his outstretched hand. Morris wrapped one free arm around Liam's waist and pulled. The captured man sprang free and the three men fell onto the hard ground. Liam knocked into Ember on the way down. They scrambled up to their feet, looking over each other quickly for injuries. Morris helped Nova to his feet, keeping his arm on him for protection. The four of them transported back to the ship just before the Oda surrounded them.

Chapter Nineteen

Nova collapsed as soon as they were safely on board. Morris helped him to a chair. Even though the green slime covered his skin, he appeared pale. His clothes were tattered and his boots looked like they were hanging on threads. He closed his eyes as Morris steadied him, taking in a sharp breath and letting it out slowly. Everyone stood silently and watched him regain his composure. In true Alexander Nova fashion, the first thing he said was a joke.

"Ew! I'm covered in that stuff! I look like someone used me as a tissue."

"Just be glad you still have a body," Morris said and handed him a towel.

Nova winced as he wiped off his face. Ember got down on a knee in front of him.

"Are you okay?"

"As good as I can be, considering I was nearly eaten."

"Bryan, set a course for Earth."

"Roger that," Morris said and headed toward the cockpit.

Liam took a seat in a chair across from them. Lewis leaned in the doorway and observed quietly. Ember looked Nova over, frowning at the damage done to his right foot.

"I guess I wasn't quick enough," she said as she began to untie his boot.

"Hey, I'm here, aren't I? It's going to take a lot more than an over-sized dessert flan to kill me."

He groaned as she pulled off his shoe. Liam turned away when he saw torn bits of flesh and purple blood peeling away as she removed his sock.

"Sorry, but this won't be for the faint of heart," she warned.

She knew it was Nova's high tolerance for pain that kept him from screaming or passing out. Still, there was no denying he was in agony. The Oda had already started to dissolve his right foot. The boot had given him some protection, but just barely. She could see the bones on the tips of his toes.

"The skin will grow back. You'll heal quickly. Question is if you want a shot for the pain or if you want to let the amethyst do its thing unobstructed?"

"No, I can handle it."

She nodded and asked Liam to hand her a medical bag from one of the equipment lockers. He gave it to her and watched as she cleaned off Nova's foot the best she could. The injured man winced and pulled his foot away.

"I'm sorry," she said. "But I have to wrap it to avoid infection."

"Do what you need to do."

She sucked on her bottom lip as she concentrated on cleaning his foot before carefully wrapping it with protective gauze.

"I think this will be all right until we get back to Earth," she said.

"Looks good."

She looked over at Lewis and raised an eyebrow. "I see you transported back in good time."

"I was going to see if I could modify the sonic emitters to send out a pulse to save Nova."

"Ah, so you weren't running."

"Of course not! Why would you suggest that?"

"I don't know. Maybe because I was busy working on freeing our friend and teammate when I noticed you were gone."

"I was working on a plan to save him. To save all of you. Why are you harping on me? I don't see you jumping on Ross's back for *not* listening to you when you told him to go back to the ship."

"Liam was helping me."

"So was I!"

"There's fear in you." Her eyes burned with intensity. "I don't know where it came from. It wasn't there before. But I can practically smell it on you now."

Fire raged in his eyes, but he didn't respond. He backed out of the doorway and disappeared. She turned her attention to Nova and completed the medical tape.

"There you are. Try to rest."

"I will."

She smiled and nodded as she stood up. She motioned for Liam to follow her out of the room when Nova's voice stopped her.

"Hey, Ember? Thanks."

"Anytime."

***

Michael Lewis sat on his bunk with his head in his hands. Everything had gone wrong. His big plan to win Ember's heart was failing. And soon, that pretty boy major would be joining their ranks. The advantages he had over Ross were dropping in numbers. He needed to figure out something, and fast.

Ember had been right when she called him a coward. She hadn't been the only one who changed. Ever since Rudo had stabbed her with the croceus-laced knife, he had been afraid. Ember had been the strongest of them all, and she had been taken down by a seemingly innocent yellow fluid.

And he'd almost lost her. When the news reached him about what had happened, he was devastated. His beautiful, fierce, proud woman was a shell of her former self. He had hoped she would open up to him, like she had before they underwent the Genesis Project. And for a little while, she did. Hope filled him for the first time, only for his fear to get in his way. So many stupid mistakes.

The idea she was in someone else's arms kept him up at night. He needed to find a way to make it right with her.

Michael rubbed his temples and laid down in the bed. His mind began to wander as he stared at the ceiling.

He always thought of her as his Ember, even though she never really belonged to him. In truth, he always believed she would never belong to anyone. And then the Major entered their lives. Ross had to go away. Permanently. There wasn't a doubt in his mind, but the question was how to do it. He could easily kill him, but if Ember found out, she would never forgive him. It was best to make it look like an accident, but it would be much more difficult now with Ross going through the Genesis. If only there was a way to ensure he wouldn't survive.

There was always the chance Ross would die naturally through the process. He wouldn't tempt fate. As bad as his luck had been lately, if he tried to do anything to the machines, it would likely make Ross better instead of killing him. Besides, he wanted a fair fight. If Ross lived, they would be on an even playing field. As much as he didn't want purple blood on his hands, it would be better for all of them that way.

Ember could never find out. He would have to lure Ross away before they went on Dr. Fergas' mission. No. It would look too suspicious if he suddenly died. He would have to kill Ross a different time, but at the first opportunity.

CHAPTER TWENTY

The flight back to Earth was quiet and uneventful. Nova's complaints when Ember made him prop his foot up and rest were silenced when she gave him a pack of gum and access to the holo network.

Every cell in her body seemed to sing with excitement when they received clearance through their planet's security shields and entered the atmosphere. They landed successfully in the ISC bay. Nova was taken to the medical center and the rest of the team headed to Dr. Fergas' office. Ember stopped in the doorway when she spotted Commander Stewart sitting next to the scientist.

"It's all right, Agent Wilson," Dr. Fergas said. "He's here in support."

"Of course I am," Commander Stewart stiffly said. "I am happy to welcome you back into the fold."

"Sure, after we did all the hard work to get here," she snapped.

"I admit my folly. I was completely wrong in my behavior. I hope you will forgive me."

"You don't know me very well if you're making a stupid statement like that."

"I understand. I just needed to make the statement."

"Covering your own ass again?"

"Always."

"I don't trust you."

"There's no reason why you should. You don't have to trust me to do your job, and that's defending this planet."

"Don't presume to tell me my duties, you pathetic little man."

He straightened his plaid necktie as the color drained from his face. He cleared his throat and tried to get back a measure of authority.

"Be careful of your words, Agent Wilson. I am the leader of the ISC, the largest governing body in the world. I am a powerful man."

"You are in control of nothing. You are a figurehead at the Grand Summit. A powerless little puppet to amuse the world leaders. You've made no changes or any significant impact during your time here. You are a joke compared to your predecessor, Commander Tennant. There is a reason why you can't even order paperclips without having to answer to the different countries on this planet. You are merely warming the seat for someone worthy. Don't think you can threaten me, *Commander*. If something were to happen to me, people would mourn. If you died, you would be replaced. Simple as that."

The venom in her voice made everyone in the room cringe. Stewart was unable to meet her gaze. Her words seemed to hang in the air. He quietly excused himself and left the room.

"Well then." Dr. Fergas wiped a bead of sweat from his brow. "Shall we get started?"

"We got what you asked for," Ember said and held up one of the containers with the purple dust in it.

"Fantastic."

He took the two containers from her and Liam and placed them on his work table. Lewis handed him the vial with the pluchiot. He put it in his pocket and began gathering various beakers of different sizes, some empty, and others with different colored liquids inside. He activated a projector and studied the formula it displayed.

"This should only take a few minutes to mix," Dr. Fergas said. "In the meantime, my assistant will prepare you."

He pressed a button on his communicuff and a woman appeared several moments later. She was tall and thin, with olive skin and long, white hair. Her lips and eyes were painted gold. Ember could make out gold tattoos on her skin.

"Hello. My name is Auna. Please follow me," she said. She motioned for them to walk through a glass door on an opposing wall, stopping Lewis as he followed. "No, not you. Only them. You are not welcomed."

"Then I'll stay here and help the doctor."

"No, we have a droid for that. You are to leave now."

"She's right, Agent Lewis," the doctor's voice rang out. "If you want to stick around, I will need you to go to the observatory window. You can't be in here."

Lewis glowered but conceded. He walked through the other door to the observation gallery.

Auna sat Ember and Liam in chairs and proceeded to take several samples of their blood. She ran through the usual battery of medical tests to check on blood sugar, heart rate, blood pressure, and respiratory. She seemed satisfied as she wrote down the numbers.

"You both are in excellent health. You should be congratulated."

"Thank you," Ember said.

They were both given a black tank top and blue shorts to wear. After they had changed, Aura led them over to the tables where they would begin the procedure. They both laid down as instructed. Auna attached the leather restraints across Ember's chest, stomach, and forehead. The wrist and leg binds were the last ones she connected. Ember hated the restraints and immediately pulled against them.

"No, it's okay. You're fine," Auna assured her.

"I know. It's just uncomfortable."

"It'll be over quickly."

The table moved so she was positioned upright. Although Ember wasn't able to turn her head, she could see Liam out of the corner of her eye.

"Liam, how are you feeling?" she called over to him and asked.

"Like my heart is going to pound out of my chest."

"Deep breaths. Don't panic."

"Right."

Auna appeared next to her and began placing tubes into her arms and legs. A chill began at the injection sites and flooded over her body. Ember closed her eyes and took in a deep breath and let it out slowly. The process would begin soon.

Auna moved over to Liam and placed the tubes on him. Dr. Fergas walked in the room, holding a long, glass cylinder filled with dark purple liquid and set it on a table. Ember smiled and watched as he grabbed another clean cylinder and poured half into it. He pulled out the vial with the pluchiot and an eye dropper. He squeezed the energy source into the dropper and placed one drop into a cylinder. The calm substance changed and began to boil. After a moment, it simmered down but Ember could see that the particles in the container were still in motion.

"It's not too late to change your mind," Dr. Fergas cautioned.

"Not on your life," she replied.

"And do you feel the same, Major Ross?"

"I do."

"I didn't think either of you would back out. Just thought I would offer."

The scientist moved out of her line of vision. Her body stiffened as a cold chill seemed to fill her veins moments later.

"What's happening?" Liam asked.

"Nothing to worry about. Just a numbing agent," Auna explained.

Ember wiggled her fingers and toes as the cold spread over her body. Moments later, the cold was replaced by heat. The temperature increased until she was sure her skin was on fire.

She cried out and pulled against her restraints. It felt like she was being stabbed with hot pokers and lightning bolts. Her body jumped and seized. Liam's cries of pain echoed hers. She clawed at the wood of the table she was strapped on. Her eyes wouldn't focus on anything. The pain was blinding her. She closed her eyes tightly and screamed. Machines began to alarm. Or maybe her ears were ringing. She could no longer be sure. Different sensations came in waves. Fire. Pain. Electricity. Pain. Her body was ready to go supernova at any moment, she was sure of it. Her body slammed against the back of the table, threatening to shatter into a million pieces.

Suddenly, her body felt heavy. It felt like an elephant was standing on her chest and she couldn't breathe. She hit the table again and didn't move. Her cries ceased, but the pain didn't subside. There was no sound in the room. No tears or screams. Not even the sound of the machines. It was dead silent.

This is it, she thought. *I'm dead.*

But the dead couldn't register pain, so she had to still be very much alive. The weight moved from her chest, allowing a rush of much needed air into her lungs. She screamed until she had no voice.

And just as quickly as it began, it was over.

The pain eased off of her. The heat followed. Another chill flooded her veins before subsiding. It took her a moment to get her bearings. She kept her eyes closed and focused. Now she could hear the sound of three people breathing. She could hear the heart racing in the person to her left as hers started to return to a normal rhythm. A whirl from a machine came to a stop. The air conditioner kicked in. She became aware of cracks on the table she was lying on. When she opened her eyes, she saw the face of Dr. Fergas smiling back at her.

"Liam?" she asked.

"He's good. Better than good. So are you. Welcome back."

***

Dr. Fergas ran another battery of tests to make sure there weren't any complications. After the assault her body had endured, all she wanted to do was take a nap. As soon as they were medically cleared, Liam and Ember disappeared back to her room. She smiled as the computer recognized her security code.

"Home sweet home," she said, motioning him inside.

"Cozy."

"Not really here much. I brought most of my personal belongings to your house."

"That is a little sad."

She shrugged. "Right now, all I care about is my bed. Would you care to join me?"

Liam grinned. "Absolutely."

She grabbed him by the arm and shoved him on the bed. They disrobed and wrestled around for position for a moment before they came to a stop on their side. She moaned as they joined together. They lost themselves in each other's bodies until they were exhausted. Ember curled up against him, resting her head on his chest.

"Is it always like this?" he asked, still slightly short of breath.

"No, normally we wouldn't get drained so quickly, but we're still recovering."

He looked at his wrist and pressed a button to display the time.

"Good Lord, woman! We've been having sex for an hour!"

"Like I said, once we've had a proper sleep, we won't get tired as easily."

She had no idea if he heard her. The rhythm of his breathing told her he was asleep. She drifted off moments later.

She was alone in the bed when she awoke. Ember sat up and looked around the room. Liam was standing in front of her full length mirror hanging on her wardrobe, looking in disbelief at his reflection.

"Morning," she greeted.

"Something like that. You realize we've slept for three days?"

"I'm not surprised. The first time I slept for four days. Your body needs time to get accustomed to everything."

"I wish Dr. Fergas would've mentioned it."

"I'm sure he thought he did. Why? You have someplace to be? Hot date?"

Liam chuckled and glanced over his shoulder at her. "Hardly. It's just surprising, that's all."

"We have a higher metabolic rate than before. The body forces you to sleep. Kinda like when you're sick and all you want to do is nap. "

"It makes sense."

Liam looked back at the mirror and tilted his head.

"What are you thinking about right now?" Ember asked.

"This is going to take some getting used to," Liam commented as he continued to stare at his reflection in the mirror.

"I know." Ember grinned. "But you will."

She walked behind him and wrapped her arms around his waist. She rested her cheek against his shoulder, peering around him to look in the mirror. His purple eyes shone brightly in the mirror. He leaned in and widened his eyes, still staring at himself in disbelief.

Ember laughed. "Purple suits you."

Liam laughed, moving his body to bring her to his side. He stroked her cheek and gazed into her purple eyes.

"You seem happy," he said.

"Incredibly, but how are you?"

"Well, I would say it's indescribable, but you understand." He smiled.

"Like you are indestructible?"

"Precisely."

"We're not, you know. We're still mortal. We can still get hurt. We will still bleed. We will still get older and one day, we will die."

"Only now we'll heal quickly, bleed purple, age slowly, and die together."

She laced her fingers with his. "That's right."

She closed her eyes and smiled. She could imagine her cells singing.

"Were you worried?" Liam asked.

"Did you forget I've been through this before?"

"No, I meant, were you worried about me?"

She scoffed. "Of course not. I knew you could handle it."

"How?"

"I chose you, remember? Well, my heart did."

Liam smiled. "I love you, too."

"So, what do you feel like?" she asked, backing away from him. "Eat, sleep, or sex?"

"Can't we do all three?"

"I wouldn't recommend it simultaneously. I really don't like integrating food play. It gets messy."

He tried to keep a straight face, but she saw his lip twitch into a smirk.

"Let's go eat," she suggested. "Then afterward, we can head to training. Let's test the limits of what we can do before we go after the time device."

CHAPTER TWENTY-ONE

They had their meal in her room. Ember sent a message to Beeka to come to her quarters. The hairdresser didn't question the directive. In fact, she didn't need any instructions. She set to work on Ember, smiling once she was done. Instead of completely dying it again, Ember decided to add black streaks to her naturally blonde hair.

"That's more like it," Ember said when she looked in the mirror. "Thank you."

"You look more like the woman Alexander told me about," she said.

"So I'm scary again?"

"No, no. Not scary. Just . . . in control."

"I appreciate that."

The other three members of Amethyst were already in the training room when they arrived. The men stopped their sparring and began to applaud.

"Look at Wilson with her purple eyes and, wow, black streaks!" Nova exclaimed. "Welcome back!"

She bowed. "Thank you, thank you."

"And you, Ross! Looking good in purple," Morris said. "Welcome to the team."

"Yeah, mate." Nova slapped him on the back. "Congratulations."

Ember looked Nova up and down. He grinned then hopped around on his feet.

"Perfectly normal and healthy, thanks to you."

"He was only off his feet for a day," Morris muttered.

"That's good to hear."

"Much to the dismay of my friend." Nova elbowed Morris in the side. "I think he was hoping it would take longer to heal."

"I'm always hoping." Morris grinned. "Longer you are gone, the longer I have peace and quiet."

Nova placed a hand over his heart and batted his eyes. "Your words wound me."

She laughed and wrapped her arms around Nova's neck, hugging him. It took him a second to hug her back.

"What's all this?" Nova asked when she pulled away. "Not that it's not nice. Just not like you."

"I'm just ridiculously happy right now."

"I'm happy too." He peered over at Liam and extended his hand. "I always knew you were good for Wilson. It's nice to see a positive change in her. Thank you."

Liam smiled as he shook Nova's hand. "I appreciate it."

"Enough with this soggy display of emotion!" Lewis blurted out. "Are we going to do something or what?"

Ember narrowed her eyes. "Fine. Let's get to it then, shall we?"

Lewis and Ember locked eyes and the others spread out. She stretched her arms out to the side, goading him on.

"No, I don't want you." Lewis shook his head.

Nova snorted. "That's a first."

"Shut up!" He turned and pointed at Liam. "I've waited a long time for this. Let's go."

"You're on." Liam shrugged off his shirt and tossed it on the floor.

"You've got to be kidding me!" Ember looked exasperatedly at them. "The first thing you want to do is fight?"

"You said it yourself before. I wasn't a match for him. I am now," Liam said.

"Unless you don't think your pretty boy could best me in a fair fight," Lewis said.

"You two want to go to blows so badly? Fine." She threw up her hands and backed out of the way. "I just want to go on record and say you both are idiots."

"Noted." Lewis nodded and he took off his shirt.

They stood toe-to-toe for several quiet moments, still sizing each other up. Lewis made the first move, punching Liam hard across the jaw. Liam didn't flinch and struck right back. He punched Lewis again, making the man stumble backward. Liam charged, but Lewis stepped out of the way, grabbing Liam by the wrist and wrenched it back. Lewis brought his elbow down on Liam's bicep. He groaned, hooking his arm with Lewis's, and flipped the other man onto his back. Lewis landed with a thud. He tried to move, but Liam kept his hold on the arm, forcing him to his feet. Lewis punched again, but Liam still didn't let go. Liam kneed Lewis into the back, and then forced him down on his knees. They traded shots until Liam let go.

Their movements became fast and furious. To ordinary eyes, they would be a blur. However, the other members could see exactly what was going on. Liam fought with precision. His training with the Air Force prepared him well. Lewis, however, behaved like a rabid animal. He hit hard, but now Liam was able to respond with the same amount of strength. Frustration was apparent on his face, and he snarled.

"You didn't set rules," Morris whispered to her.

"What?"

"You didn't set rules for the spar. They have no reason to stop before someone gets hurt or killed."

"Liam wouldn't intentionally hurt Lewis."

"Not intentionally, no, but he doesn't know his own strength right now," Nova whispered.

"And would you stand there and tell me Lewis wouldn't kill Liam if he had the chance?" Morris asked.

"Michael wouldn't kill him," Ember scoffed at the notion.

"He'd do anything for you."

She studied Morris for a moment, trying to gauge his facial expression. She looked back at the skirmish just as Lewis kicked Liam in the back of the head. Liam stumbled forward, but managed to avoid Lewis attempting to jump on his back. He kicked Lewis in the ribs, hard enough to hear ribs crack. He automatically dropped out of his defensive stance.

"Oh, man, I'm sorry. I didn't mean —"

Lewis lunged at Liam and wrapped his hands around his throat. Ember wasted no time in rushing over and pulled Lewis off. He growled and sputtered, only stopping when he saw her face.

"What the hell were you thinking?" she asked.

When he didn't answer, she decked him across the jaw. Lewis fell into a heap on the floor. Satisfaction filled her when she saw the telltale sign of a purple blood trail on the corner of his mouth. He took the full force of her second blow, crumpling to the ground again. She stood over him, daring him with her body language to say or do anything.

Nova helped Liam to his feet. Visible bruising was around his neck. Both men were bleeding from their nose. Lewis grimaced as he stood tall, placing a hand over his ribs. Ember touched Liam's arm, but he waved his hand, letting her know he was all right. Her eyes blazed as she turned her attention to Lewis.

"What was going through your head, hm? He said he was sorry. He doesn't know his strength yet, he didn't mean it."

"I got into the fight and I lost it. I'm sorry," Lewis said, shrugging his shoulders.

"Damn right you lost it! You would've killed him if I hadn't stopped you."

"Ember, it's okay," Liam said, walking beside her and touching her arm.

"How can you say it's okay? It's not!"

"It was the heat of the moment. It's already forgiven."

"I don't believe this. Lewis, give me one good reason why I shouldn't bring you up on charges right now."

Lewis glowered. "Because if I intended to kill him, I wouldn't do it in front of you. And had I murdered him in cold blood, I would expect you to kill me next. I'm not in favor of dying. And I don't want blood spilt."

She looked at Lewis and back and Liam. Liam nodded, wiping the purple blood from his face.

"See? I'm already healing, Ember," Liam calmly said.

"I wish I could believe you," she muttered, keeping her eyes locked on Lewis.

"Ember, I'm fine," Liam insisted. "Better than fine, really. Let's just move past this."

"Can you both agree that this is over and not pull some stupid stunt again? I can't have this weighing on my mind while we are out on missions."

"Absolutely," Liam quickly replied.

He extended out his hand toward Lewis. Ember raised an eyebrow as Lewis accepted it.

"Of course. We're a team now. I'm going to start acting like it."

"Thank you. Both of you."

***

Ember still wasn't sure if she believed Lewis or not, but felt like she should give him the benefit of doubt. After everything they had been through, it was the least she could do. She just wished she understood his behavior.

"I understand," Liam said when she mentioned it to him as they were gearing up to leave. "This is an act of a desperate man."

"Desperate man?"

"You have no idea the affect you have on people, Ember. Nova and Morris think of you as a sister. They would give their lives for you. I can see the respect and admiration shining in their eyes. With Lewis, there's something beyond that. He loves you. In his eyes, I am the enemy standing between what he wants, which is a life with you."

"See, it's hard for me to grasp that. I've never told him anything to indicate that. If it wasn't for you, he and I would be together."

"I believe you, but when I wasn't around, you did sleep with him."

"That was just sex. It was control. At least, it was initially." She paused when he narrowed his eyes. "Okay, and maybe it did turn into a situation for comfort."

"Exactly. Ember, you aren't exactly the type who turns to someone for comfort. You reached out for him in need and it was more than just physical."

He was right. She closed her eyes and swore under her breath. *Is Liam right? Did I lead Lewis on?*

She sighed. "What can I do to fix this?"

"It'll be okay. He'll get over it."

"I hope so."

***

Michael Lewis banged his head on the table in his quarters, cursing at himself. He had lost control during the fight with Ross. There was no denying that. Ember had nearly broken his jaw with her punches, not that he blamed her. He was surprised she didn't completely take his head off.

He couldn't deny her feelings for Ross. He hated to admit it, but he was beginning to like Ross. He made Ember happier than he could ever recall seeing her. He never backed down and he could handle himself in a fight. Maybe he had misjudged Ross.

All right, so maybe the man didn't have to die. That didn't mean he was going to give up on Ember. No, he still had a plan. If it failed, he could say he'd given it everything he had and he would back off. But he didn't think it would fail.

All it needed was a little finesse.

CHAPTER TWENTY-TWO

Before all five members of Amethyst could leave on their mission, Liam had one more stop he had to make. He had officially moved out of his apartment on base and into new living arrangements on the ISC. Ember didn't ask, she just moved the few belongings she had in. Not that he minded.

He donned his Air Force blues for the last time and stood in front of General Tom Blanchard. The General held a bland expression, but Liam could see the smile in his eyes.

"Major Liam Ross, on this day, you are hereby stripped of all rights, privileges, and rank provided to you by the Global United Air Force." He reached over and removed the stripes on Liam's shoulder. "You are officially removed from your access clearance and pay grade. Effective immediately, you are now honorably discharged from active service."

"Sir?" Liam blinked.

"You are not being discharged for misconduct, and you aren't on active discipline. Yours is voluntary. There is no punishment being inflicted here."

The general was giving him a window. If something were to happen with Amethyst or the ISC, he could reenlist.

Ember had received a dishonorable discharge when she joined the Genesis Project.

"I was angry when she left," Blanchard said, as if reading Liam's thoughts. "I acted out in pain. I'll always be sorry for my past with my daughter."

"Is this your way of making up for it?"

"Maybe a little. I doubt I'll fully be forgiven in her eyes, but we're working on having a relationship. Still, you deserve to leave with your head held high. Your service record is exemplary and you should be praised. Go on. Start your new life."

They shook hands. Liam's heart swelled with pride.

"Thank you, sir."

"I don't need to tell you to look after Ember."

"I think she's more than capable of taking care of herself."

"She is. No doubt she can take care of the world too. Still, whether she wants to admit it or not, she needs someone. And I'm glad that someone is you."

"Wow." Liam's words caught in his throat. "That means . . ."

"You're like the son I never had, Liam. I am incredibly proud of the man you've become. Your father would be too."

A tear rolled down his cheek. Liam quickly wiped it away and nodded.

"Coming from you, sir, that means the world to me. Thank you."

"No, thank you, son. Call me if you ever need anything."

"I will."

***

"There he is!" Nova exclaimed as Liam approached the team in the ISC hangar. "We were worried we'd have to leave without you."

"No, we weren't." Ember shook her head. "How did it go?"

He had already changed out of his blues and was now dressed in the ISC's black uniform. He straightened his belt and nodded.

"Very well. I was given an honorable discharge."

Surprise filled her eyes. "That's better than I expected."

"General Blanchard is not an unreasonable man."

"No, never to you." She frowned. "Still, it's good news. Are you ready?"

"Good to go. Are we?"

"Lewis got the coordinates for the planet and the dummy device from Dr. Fergas. We're all set."

"Excellent. Let's get under way."

The team boarded their ship. Nova received clearance and they left Earth.

"Where are we headed?" Liam asked.

"The Bramley System," Ember replied.

"Bramley? I thought that system was dead."

"Essentially, yes. None of the planets in the solar system have any life."

"That's where the danger comes into play," Lewis said.

"Danger from a dead planet," Liam blandly said.

"The entire system was once brimming with life. Three planets with millions of inhabitants each. However, the Solarians took care of that."

Liam frowned. The Solarians were a species who lived inside stars across the universe. They believed they were superior and undefeatable. The only time they left their celestial bodies was to cause devastation and mayhem on worlds they felt needed to be destroyed. Earth history states after the war with the Synth, the Solarians came to the planet. They had dismissed Earth until they witnessed the strength and technology it possessed. They would've claimed Earth as theirs had it not been for Dr. Mackenzie Rhodes coming up with new technology which proved they could be defeated. The Solarians went back into the Sun and left the planet alone.

Liam had heard of the Solarians being merciful if it suited them. Stories ranged from burning all life on one half of a planet to only killing a third of a population.

"I wonder what these planets did to deserve complete eradication in the Solarians's eyes," Liam muttered.

"Who knows, mate? I just consider ourselves lucky to have never faced them," Nova said.

"I think it'll be fascinating," Morris said. "We still have the weapon created by Dr. Rhodes."

"That's the only reason they haven't attacked," Ember pointed out. "I would prefer to never face a sun creature."

Liam nodded in agreement. Even with his new abilities, he didn't know how he would fight a being made of energy with no solid form.

It would take four days with their advanced engines to enter Bramley space. Thankfully, it was uneventful. They spent their time playing cards and watching holo shows. Ember was happy and amazed to see Liam and Lewis actually getting along, even laughing together. She relaxed. Maybe the animosity between them had passed.

It should be a simple mission. They had the coordinates where the time device was buried. They would beam down near the site and dig. An easy swap with the fake device created by Dr. Fergas and they would be headed back to Earth.

As they gathered their sonic shovels, Lewis tapped Ember on the shoulder. "Can I talk to you alone for a moment?"

She looked at him strangely but nodded. She followed him into the sleeping quarters. He shut the door behind them.

"You are acting funny. What's wrong?"

"I just wanted to talk to you for a moment."

"Right now? We're transporting to the surface."

"I know, but just hear me out, all right?"

She sighed and frowned. Now wasn't the time for this, but she didn't think he would let it go until he had said what was on his mind. She shrugged, waving her arms to the side.

"I'm not going to express my heart. You already know what's inside of me. But you're happy with him. There's no denying it."

"I really am."

"You deserve happiness. But there is one thing I want you to consider."

"What's that?"

"Me."

She shoved against his chest and scoffed.

"I mean it. I know you want him, but there's a part of you that's never stopped wanting me. You can deny it all you want, but you've never closed your heart to me. I'm like a shadow, floating around in your head and heart."

"I think you're full of yourself."

"There is going to come a time when you need to make a choice."

"I've already made my choice."

"No, you haven't. If you had, I wouldn't be able to do this."

Without a warning, Lewis kissed her. Surprise rippled through her body. Before she could protest, he wrapped his arms around her and deepened the kiss. Her body responded to him without thought. She gave in to the moment. The intensity of their kiss increased and she whimpered slightly when he broke their embrace. Lewis pressed his forehead against hers and ran his thumb across her cheek.

"You can't deny that."

And with that, he was gone. Ember's heart raced against her rib cage as she struggled to regain some of her composure. She walked into the bathroom and splashed water on her face. Guilt washed over her as she met up with the team.

Liam looked at her curiously. "Are you okay?"

"Why wouldn't I be?"

He didn't look convinced but didn't press the issue. She let out a sigh of relief and grabbed a bag with the digging equipment. The five of them transported down to the surface of the dead planet.

The sky was grey even though the planet was unnaturally warm. Without wind, the air was stagnant. Sulfur filled her nostrils as she dug into the blackened dirt.

"How far do we have to dig?" Morris asked.

"Three feet," Lewis replied.

Ember's mind began to wander as they dug. She tried to press the image of their kiss out of her mind, but she couldn't. Was Lewis right? Should she tell Liam? If it was only a kiss, there was no reason to. It would only upset him. The problem was, she couldn't answer if it was only a kiss.

The planet was hotter than she expected. Sweat clung to their bodies and got in their eyes. Liam stopped to swipe the sweat away.

"Uh, what's that?" Liam asked.

"What?" Ember asked.

"That." Liam pointed up at the sky.

Ember looked up to see what looked like a shooting star flash across the sky. Another one followed, only it touched down on the ground several feet from them.

"Time to go!"

The device started to show through the dirt. Ember and Lewis got down on their knees and began to dig with their hands. The others quickly joined them, and soon, a piece of shiny metal became more visible.

The time device was oddly shaped. There were four panels in the shape of triangles coming to a point. It sat on a platform that housed many different shaped circular buttons. They managed to pull it free from the earth as the stars fell closer to them. Ember grabbed the device and got on her feet. Nova and Morris beamed back to the ship. She moved to activate her wrist transporter module, but a strong force from behind knocked her forward. She cradled the device to her chest as she crashed on the ground.

"Ember!" Liam grabbed her by the arm to help her to her feet.

"I'm okay."

The temperature seemed to rise as the sky lit up with stars. After a moment, Ember realized it wasn't stars, but fireballs. A streak of fire began pouring down on them. They rolled out of the way, dodging several of them.

Much to her amazement, the device started to grow hot. Small lights lit up on the side. She had to roll again to avoid another fire blast, dropping the device in the process. Buttons on it lit up and the four panels started to pull apart. Smoke poured from the center and a beam of light shot up to the sky. She reached for the device and the smoke moved toward her. It enveloped her hand, moving up her arm. She tried to shake it off, but it kept coming. The skin beneath began to tingle. A bright flash of light blinded her.

Suddenly, there was a sensation of the ground giving away beneath her. Everything disappeared. She couldn't see anything but the light. Nothing made sense to her. She had no sense of direction or of her surroundings.

The next thing she knew, she was gone. She gasped as she stood firm on her feet and looked around. She wasn't sure what had happened, but she was no longer on the planet. She didn't know where Liam and Lewis were, and she wasn't in a room she recognized. The walls were bare except for a few pictures near two office desks in the upper right hand corner of the room. There were two long, black laboratory tables in the middle of the room. She was standing on one side of a table. Opposite of her were two women, staring at her with open jaws and wide eyes.

They were the same height and build. One woman had long blonde hair and light blue eyes. The other had short, spiky blonde hair and dark blue eyes. Their faces were nearly identical. Ember could hardly believe her eyes.

"No, it can't be." Ember shook her head.

"I'm sorry, but where did you come from?" the woman with the long hair asked.

"Yeah, you just appeared out of nowhere," the other said.

"I've got to be dreaming. This isn't possible," Ember said.

"What isn't possible?"

"Are you Dr. Madison Brooks?"

The woman blinked several times. "I am. What's your name?"